Heinrich Heine

Heine on Shakespeare

A translation of his notes on Shakespeare heroines

Heinrich Heine

Heine on Shakespeare
A translation of his notes on Shakespeare heroines

ISBN/EAN: 9783337214104

Printed in Europe, USA, Canada, Australia, Japan

Cover: Foto ©Andreas Hilbeck / pixelio.de

More available books at **www.hansebooks.com**

HEINE ON SHAKESPEARE

HEINE ON SHAKESPEARE

A TRANSLATION OF HIS
NOTES ON SHAKESPEARE HEROINES

By

IDA BENECKE

" Thy greatest knew thee, Mother Earth; unsoured
He knew thy sons. He probed from hell to hell
Of human passions, but of love deflowered
His wisdom was not, for he knew thee well."
—GEORGE MEREDITH.

WESTMINSTER
ARCHIBALD CONSTABLE
AND CO. 1895

TRANSLATOR'S NOTE

THE following pages, written in 1838, owe their origin to some English engravings of Shakespeare Heroines which had attracted Heine's notice. He thought more highly of the illustrations than of his own words concerning the heroines they were intended to pourtray. Nevertheless Heine's work has outlived the fancy portraits which called it forth, and may well be studied by those who have a mind to open their Shakespeare.

CONTENTS

CONTENTS

HEINE ON SHAKESPEARE

I know a good Hamburg Christian who could never get over the fact that our Lord and Saviour was by birth a Jew. It distressed him greatly when forced to admit that this praiseworthy and perfect Man actually belonged to the company of unclean long-noses, who idle about the streets, who merit all his disdain, and who are specially odious to him when, like himself, they become wholesale dealers in spices and tobacco, and cause the price of his goods to fall in the market.

Even as Jesus Christ impressed this son of Hamonia, so am I impressed by William Shakespeare. I grow desperate when I reflect that after all he is an Englishman, belonging to that most odious nation which God in his anger created.

It is an odious nation, a joyless country, stiff, old-fashioned, selfish, narrow, English! Father Ocean would long since have swallowed up this nation, had he not feared the sea-sickness which might thereupon ensue . . . this nation, grey and yawning as a monster, breathing forth naught but suffocation and deadly tedium, which will probably eventually hang itself by means of a huge cable.

And in such a country, issuing from such a nation, William Shakespeare first saw the light of day in April, 1564.

But the England of those days, the birthplace of the man born in that northern Bethlehem called Stratford-on-Avon, to whom we owe the gospel of this our world, as we may well name the Plays of Shakespeare — the England of those days must surely have differed widely from the England of this. Indeed they called it *Merry England*, and it was bright with many colours, fanciful costumes, profound whimsicality, teeming energy, exuberant passions. . . . Life there was a bright tournament, where well-born knights played the first part in weal and woe, but where the hearts of the people also beat in unison with the merry trumpet sound. . . . //In place of strong beer people drank light wine, that democratic beverage which by its inebriating effect equalises all who by position and birth stand apart from one another on the dull stage of reality./

All this brilliant merriment has faded away since then, the glad trumpet-sounds have ceased, the fine intoxication is past . . . and the nation holds in its hands yon book called the Plays of William Shakespeare as a comfort for bad times and as a proof that *Merry England* did actually once exist.

It is a blessing that Shakespeare came in the nick of time, and that he was contemporary with Elizabeth and James. Owing to the impulse given by protestantism thought was free and unhampered, whilst customs and beliefs remained unchanged. Though protestantism encouraged unlimited freedom of thought, manners and beliefs were not affected thereby, and the sunset of chivalry still glowed over that kingdom which was encircled by a halo of glorious poetry. Indeed Catholicism, the national creed of the Middle Ages, was destroyed only in theory, it still exerted its magic influence over the minds of men, and swayed their manners, customs and beliefs. Only later on, the puritans succeeded in rooting up blossom by blossom the religion of the past, investing the country with that barren spirit of melancholy like a cloud of grey fog, which sank at last into a lukewarm whining and restless pietism, for very lack of life. Just as religion still maintained its old form, so also the British monarchy of Shakespeare's time had not yet undergone that sickly change which goes by the name of Constitutionalism — a form of government by no means favourable to art, though it may be favourable to European liberty. With the death of Charles, England's last true and great king, English poetry ceased to exist, and the poet was thrice happy not to have experienced this miserable event, of which possibly he had a presentiment. Shakespeare is often called an aristocrat. I do not wish to contradict this ; indeed his political views are excusable when we remember how he, with his prophetic insight, could fix upon certain signs of the time, predicting that levelling puritanic age, which, besides destroying the monarchy, would make an end of all joy, all poetry, all genial art.

Indeed, during the reign of the puritans, art was proscribed in England ; the zeal of protestantism was specially directed against the stage, and Shakespeare's very name was forgotten by the English for many years. The expressions of anger contained in the pamphlets of that time astonish us, viz., in the *Histrio Mastix* of the celebrated Prynne, in which he anathematises the stage in screeching tones. Are the

puritans to be very seriously blamed for their
zeal ? Ah no ! in history, all who remain true
to their convictions are right, and these dismal
Roundheads only acted in obedience to that
spirit, intolerant of everything connected with
art, which manifested itself as early as the first
centuries of the Church, and continues down to
this day in iconoclastic guise. This old impla-
cable aversion to everything connected with the
stage is nothing more than one side of that
hostility which has raged between two hetero-
geneous views for the last eighteen hundred
years. One opinion had its origin in the barren
soil of Judæa, the other in the fair fields of
Greece. Ah yes ! this hatred between Jerusalem and Athens, between the holy shrine and
the cradle of art, between life in the soul and
the soul in life, has continued for the past
eighteen hundred years ; and the quarrels, the
public and private wars of which it has been
the cause become manifest to the esoteric
student in the history of mankind. When we
read in to-day's newspapers that a poor dead
actor is refused the ordinary rites of burial by
the Archbishop of Paris, we cannot attribute
this to the special whim of an ecclesiastic, and
only the shortsighted will construe it as narrow-
minded malice. We see in this rather the

earnestness of an old strife, of a death-struggle against art, turned by the Hellenic spirit into a platform from which to preach the laws of life, as opposed to soul-deadening Judaism. By its persecution of actors the Church made war on the representatives of Greece ; and the poets also, who attributed their divine inspiration to Apollo, making the land of poetry a harbour of refuge for the outlawed divinities ·of heathen-dom, frequently had to suffer a similar persecution. Or is there perhaps some malicious feeling at the bottom of this ? During the first two centuries actors were the most intolerant enemies of the oppressed church, and the *Acta Sanctorum* often inform us that these godless actors spent their time in performing on the' Roman stage parodies of the manner of life and miracles of the Nazarene as an amusement for the heathen populace. Or had this bitter strife between the servants of spiritual and temporal creeds its root in mutual jealousy ?

Next to ascetic zeal we find that republican fanaticism called forth in the puritans hatred for the Old-English stage. Here royalism and noble houses, as well as heathenism and heathen opinions, had their praises sung. I have shown elsewhere how much the puritans of old and the republicans of to-day resemble one another

in this respect.[1]   May Apollo and the everlasting Muses save us from the dominion of
these last!

The name of Shakespeare was forgotten for
a long period, during the turmoil of these forenamed ecclesiastic and political revolutions, and
nearly a century elapsed before he was again
held in esteem.   After that period however
his fame increased from day to day, and he
beamed like a spiritual sun over that country
which is sunless for nearly twelve months of
the year, that island of darkness, that Botany
Bay minus a southern climate, that smoky,
machine-whirring, church-going and wine-bib-
bing England.   Good Mother Nature never
completely disinherits her children, and whilst
she has withheld from Englishmen all beautiful
and lovely things, giving them neither a voice
for song nor senses for enjoyment, perhaps
even endowing them with wrinkled pot-bellies
instead of human souls, she has given them
instead considerable civic freedom, the talent of
making themselves comfortable in their homes,
and William Shakespeare!

Yes!   He is the spiritual sun, shining upon
that land with warm and beneficent beams.

---

[1] Viz., characters in *Julius Cæsar* in the following pages.

Everything there reminds us of Shakespeare, and what a halo is thrown by him over the commonest things! Everywhere the enveloping wings of his genius enfold us ; his clear eye seems to beam forth on us from every striking countenance we see, and on occasions of great public interest we fancy we perceive him silently nodding to us with an expressive smile.

I became especially aware of the constant homage paid to Shakespeare during my stay in London while running about all day to gaze upon the so-called *sights* — every *lion* called to mind the greater lion—Shakespeare. His historical plays have immortalised all the places I visited, which were thus familiar to me from my earliest childhood. Not only the educated man, but every man of the people in England is conversant with Shakespeare. Even the stout beef-eater at the tower with his red coat and his red face, pointing out the dungeon at the back of the central gateway where Richard ordered his nephews the young princes to be murdered, reminds us of Shakespeare who has given us a further account of this sad story. The Sacristan at Westminster Abbey also constantly alludes to Shakespeare, in whose tragedies those dead kings and queens play such a miserable part, and who repose here on their tombs in counterfeit of stone and are shown for eighteenpence. The statue of the great poet himself stands there in life-size representing a striking man with thoughtful brow, holding in his hands a roll of parchment . . . Possibly magic words are written there, and when he moves his white lips at midnight, calling on the dead who repose in their tombs, they come forth in rusty armour and faded court-dress, these knights of the white and the red roses, and the ladies also rise with a sob from their resting-place, and there is a clashing of swords, a laughing and a cursing. Just as at Drury Lane, where I often saw the plays of Shakespeare, when Kean caused me deep emotion as he ran despairingly across the stage, crying out:

" A horse, a horse, my kingdom for a horse ! "

Were I to name all the places which reminded me of Shakespeare, I should have to copy out the entire *Guide to London*. Especially in the Houses of Parliament did I feel this to be the case, not on account of Westminster Hall, so frequently mentioned by Shakespeare, but on account of the debates I heard there. Here Shakespeare was frequently mentioned, as well as passages quoted from his works, on account of their historical and not their poetic importance. I was amazed to find that in England Shakespeare is not only looked upon in the light of a poet, but that he is regarded as a historian by influential statesmen and Members of Parliament.

I here observe that it would be foolish to look for precisely that kind of interest in Shakespeare's historical plays which could only be supplied by a dramatist whose highest aim is the clever manipulation of poetry. Shakespeare's aim was not only poetry, but history; he could not model his given subject-matter at will, he could not follow his fancy in describing events and characters, and as little as he could observe unity of time and place could he merge his entire interest in a single person or a single event. And yet in his historical plays we find richer, more powerful, and sweeter poetry than in the tragedies of those poets who either invent their own stories, or arrange them as suits their taste, whereby they obtain the strictest symmetry of form and surpass poor Shakespeare in art properly so-called, especially in the *enchaînement des scènes.*

Yes, it is a significant fact; the great Englishman is not only a poet but also a historian

—he wields the sharp style of Klio as well as Melpomene's dagger. In this he resembles the earliest historians who likewise made no difference between poetry and history, and who not only gave a nomenclature to the past issuing in a dusty collection of events, but made truth more beautiful by song, producing from this harmony only the notes of truth. So-called objectivity, of which we now hear so much, is nothing but a tiresome lie; we cannot depict the past without giving it the colour of our feelings. And as the so-called objective historian always addresses the present generation, he writes unconsciously in the spirit of his own times, and this spirit of the times will become manifest in his works. In the interchange of epistolary correspondence we detect in like manner the characters of recipient and correspondent. So-called objectivity, proudly passive, taking its stand on the golgotha of events, may be regarded as untrue, because we not only require an accurate summary of facts in dealing with historic truth, but also a certain description of the impression made on contemporaries by such events. Yet herein lies the difficulty; for we want more than an ordinary enumeration of events, we need the capacity of a poet to whom, Shakespeare says—*the very eye and body of the time*—have become manifest.

And not only the occurrences of his own time were manifest to him, but those which are contained in ancient records. We have a striking example of this in those tragedies where he gives us so true an account of Rome in its decay. Not only has he portrayed the knights of the Middle Ages ; he has seen into the hearts of ancient heroes, drawing forth from them their inmost thoughts. He could always turn truth into poetry, and knew how to cast a poetic halo over the heartless Romans, this hard cold and prosaic nation, made up of vulgar greed and clever astuteness, a nation of casuistic soldiery.

But Shakespeare is stigmatised as wanting in *form*, even in his Roman tragedies. A talented writer, Dietrich Grabbe, called them *poetically adorned chronicles* wanting in every point of central interest, in which we fail to perceive who play the important and who the unimportant parts, and in which, though we may dispense with unity of time and place, there is not even unity of action. But the cleverest critics make strange mistakes ! Not only the last named unity, but unities of time and place are by no means wanting in the great poet, only his conceptions are somewhat more elastic than ours. This world forms the stage, of his plays, and that is his unity of place; eternity is the period during which his plays come to pass, and that is his unity of time; and the hero of his plays, the bright central figure, representing the unity of action and comformable to the other two, is—Mankind; a hero who is always dying and always rising again, always loving, always hating, yet in whom love is stronger than hate; now crawling like a worm, now soaring like an eagle, now deserving a fool's cap, now a laurel-wreath, or still oftener both of these at one and the same time; the great dwarf, the small giant, the homœopathically prepared divinity, in whom the divine elements may have become diluted, but which exist nevertheless. Ah! let us not overrate the heroism of this hero, for the sake of modesty and very shame!

Shakespeare is as true to nature as he is faithful in delineating history. It is often said that he holds up a mirror to nature. This is not correct, as these words convey a wrong impression concerning the relations in which a poet stands to nature. Nature is not reflected in the poet's mind; he is endowed with the innate capacity for representing nature, which representation is akin to the most faithful reflection ; he comes into the world a world-wise man, and every part of the external world is immediately understood by him in its entirety when he awakens from the dreams of his childhood and attains to a knowledge of himself. For his mind bears an impress of the whole, he knows the ultimate reasons of all phenomena, which to the ordinary mind appear problematic, and which to the ordinary investigator seem difficult, if not impossible of solution . . . Just as the mathematician can immediately explain the whole circle and its centre, if he is shown the smallest part of a circle, so also the poet, in the very act of contemplating the infinitesimal part of objective things, realises the connection between this part and all other things. He seems to know the circle of things and their centre, he sees things in their widest dimensions and to the inmost core.

But before the poet awakens to this marvellous comprehension he must always be brought in contact with some portion of the objective world. This perception of a fragment of the phenomenal world is reached by means of his senses, and it forms as it were the outward event, determining those inward revelations of which his works are the result. And the greater the poet, the more is our curiosity excited concerning those external occurrences which first called his works into being. We like to hunt up the actual facts of a poet's life. This curiosity is all the more foolish, as according to what was previously stated, the importance of external occurrences bears no proportion to the importance of the creations, emanating from them. These occurrences may be, and usually are, as trivial and insignificant as the poet's life ordinarily is. I say trivial and insignificant, for I will not make use of sadder words. Poets present themselves to the world through the halo of their works, and when looked at from afar, they dazzle us by their glory. Let us never inspect their lives too closely! We may compare them to those bright beacons, shining athwart lawn and bower, which we take for the stars of the world . . . for diamonds and emeralds, costly jewels, which kings' children, playing in the garden, have hung on to the shrubs and then forgotten . . . for bright dew-drops which have rolled away into the high grass, and are now refreshing themselves in the cool night-air, sparkling with joy, until the approach of day, when the rosy dawn draws them back into herself. . . . Ah! let us not seek the track of these stars, jewels and dewdrops by the light of day! In their stead we shall perceive a poor discoloured worm, crawling miserably across our path, hateful to look upon, and yet which, owing to a curious feeling of pity, we refrain from crushing!

In what did the private life of Shakespeare consist? Little concerning him has come to light in spite of enquiry, and this is a blessing; only a few unproven, stupid stories concerning the poet's youth and life have been handed down to us. He is said to have killed the sheep of his father, who was a butcher. . . . Perhaps from these were descended those English commentators who possibly out of spite taxed him with ignorance and a general infringement of the rules of art in his works. Others describe him as a wool-stapler, who failed in business. . . . Poor fellow, he probably thought that by becoming a wool-stapler he would at last be in luck's way. I believe nothing of all this, it ends in much cry and little wool. I am more inclined to think that the great poet went in for poaching, getting into trouble through deer-stalking, for which I cannot utterly condemn him.—*Even Master Honest once stole a calf*, says a German proverb.—On this they say he fled to

London, where for a small fee he took charge of great people's horses at the theatre doors. . . . In some such guise are shaped the legends which one stupid old woman gets from another, and which are frequently met with in the history of literature.

In Shakespeare's sonnets we have an authentic record of the events of his life. These I would rather not discuss on account of the acute human misery therein displayed, which occasioned my previous remarks concerning the poet's private life.

We can easily explain the want of trustworthy data concerning Shakespeare's life, when we remember the political and ecclesiastical struggles which occurred soon after his death. For a space of time these brought about a positive puritan rule, the unpleasant effects of which continued even down to a later time, and which not only destroyed but brought into sheer oblivion the Elizabethan golden age of English literature. When at the commencement of last century Shakespeare's works again came to light, commentators had no reliable material on which to base their conclusions. For these they had to fall back on shallow empiricism, if not on more pitiable materialism. With the exception of William Hazlitt, England has produced no Shakespearian critic of any importance. Everywhere we find trifle-mongering, egotistic shallowness, conceited enthusiasm, and learned inflation which threatens to burst with joy when it traces any antiquarian, geographical or chronological mistake in the poor poet, and which makes it matter for regret that he did not study the ancients in their mother tongue and that his education had been neglected. For he makes the Romans wear hats, makes ships land in Bohemia, and quotes Aristotle contemporaneously with the Trojan war! This was past the endurance of a learned English professor, who had graduated as M.A. at Oxford. The forenamed Hazlitt is the only Shakespearian critic who forms an exception and who is pre-eminent in every way. His mind was as brilliant as it was deep, a combination of Diderot and Börne, full of warm enthusiasm for the Revolution, coupled with an earnest love of art, always overflowing with *verve* and *esprit*!

Germans have entered into the mind of Shakespeare better than Englishmen. I will first mention our favourite Gotthold Ephraim Lessing, always foremost in setting a good example. He was the first German who raised his voice in favour of Shakespeare.

He laid the weightiest foundation-stone of a temple erected in honour of the greatest of all poets ; and more than this,—he carefully cleared the ground, on which this temple was to be erected, of its former rubbish. The lightly constructed French booths, proudly exhibiting their wares on that ground, were mercilessly torn down by him in his architectural zeal. Gottsched shook the curls of his wig so despairingly that the town of Leipzig quaked, and the cheeks of his spouse grew white with fear, or was this achieved by means of a powder-puff? We may say that Lessing's entire *Dramaturgie* was written to glorify Shakespeare.

After Lessing comes Wieland. He succeeded, by means of his translations, in bringing about in Germany a better understanding of the great poet's works. The author of *Agathon and Musarion*, the playful *cavaliere servente* of the Graces, became suddenly so impressed with English earnestness that he was the man who sang the praises of that very hero who was to conduce to his own downfall.

Herder was the third great German who sang the enthusiastic praises of Shakespeare. Goethe also did him homage with a great flourish of trumpets; in short, there was a whole race of kings, who one after the other cast in their vote for William Shakespeare, electing him as the emperor-king of literature.

This emperor-king was already firmly seated on his throne, when the good knight August Wilhelm von Schlegel, with his squire, Hofrath Ludwig Tieck, bent down in homage before him, assuring all the world that now the kingdom was secure and that the millennium of the great William Shakespeare had come.

Were I to overlook the great service which A. W. Schlegel has rendered by means of his translation of Shakespeare's Plays and of his readings of the same, I should be guilty of injustice. But actually there is in the latter a want of philosophical substructure, they are pervaded apparently by a frivolous dilettantism, and I cannot praise them unreservedly, on account of several ugly and conspicuous *arrière-pensées*. The enthusiasm of A. W. Schlegel is always artificial, an intentionally self-deceptive fit of intoxication, and with him, as with other writers of the romantic school, Shakespeare's apotheosis was intended indirectly to contribute towards Schiller's degradation. Schlegel's translation has so far certainly been the most successful, and it follows the rules of a metrical rendering. The feminine character of his genius is here of great use to the translator, and he is able in his colourless cleverness to lean on another mind in all love and fidelity.

I confess, however, that notwithstanding these virtues I am often inclined to place Eschenburg's translation, done entirely in prose, higher, and for the following reasons ; — the language used by Shakespeare is not peculiar to him, it has come down to him from his forefathers and contemporaries, and it is the language which the dramatic writers of that time had to make use of, whether it suited their taste or not. We need only skim Dodsley's collection of old plays to notice a similar kind of language in all the tragedies and comedies of that time ; the same eupheuism, exaggerated delicacy, artificial word-structure, the same conceits, play upon words and bombastic expressions which we find in Shakespeare and which stupid people blindly admire. But the understanding reader when he does not blame them, only excuses them on the plea of their being an excrescence, a necessary condition of the times. But Shakespeare divests himself of this traditional stage-language, and shows himself as he is ; grandly beautiful, with a simplicity which vies with unadulterated nature, delighting us strangely in those portions of his writings where his fullest genius is displayed, and in which he gives vent to his highest inspirations. Indeed in such passages Shakespeare has a certain peculiarity even in his language, which can never be faithfully rendered by the metrical translator, who with bound feet limps along in pursuit of the thought. In the ordinary routine language of the stage, these remarkable passages are lost sight of by the metrical translator, and even Schlegel cannot escape this fate. But why trouble about a metrical translation if it does away with the best part of a poet's work, giving us only that which is imperfect? A prose translation which can produce better the unostentatious and natural purity of certain passages is therefore really preferable to a metrical rendering.

Following closely on Schlegel, L. Tieck has done some good work as an exponent of Shakespeare. This was principally by means of his *Dramaturgische Blätter* which appeared in the *Abend-Zeitung*, fourteen years ago, and which created considerable sensation among actors and playgoers. Unfortunately this *amiable scamp*, as Gutzkow called him, took secret pleasure in adopting a tone of vague tedious sermonising in these papers. He made up for his ignorance of the classics and even of philosophy, in decorum and solemnity, and we might fancy ourselves in the presence of Sir John Falstaff lecturing the prince. But in spite of the bombastic and pedagogic gravity with which the little man endeavours to hide his philological and philosophical ignorance, we find some extremely clever remarks concerning Shakespeare's heroes in these papers, and here and there we trace that poetic feeling, which we always admired and gladly acknowledged in Tieck's former writings.

Ah, this Tieck! who was once a poet, and might be considered as one of the most aspiring if not one of the greatest; how is he fallen! What a miserably curtailed pittance does he now offer us annually, compared to the liberal creations of his muse in the early days of tender legendary lore. Much as we once loved, do we now hate this envious weakling, who slanders the high-souled sorrows of German youth in his gossiping novels. To him we might apply Shakespeare's words:

> " For sweetest things turn sourest by their deeds,
> Lilies that fester smell far worse than weeds."

Franz Horn must be named among the great poet's commentators. His expositions of

Shakespeare are the most complete, and occupy five volumes. They are not wanting in
soul, but it is such a faded, rarefied soul
that the most soulless stupidity would be
preferable. It is strange that this man, who
devoted all his life to the study of Shakespeare
and ardently admired him, was a weak-minded
pietist. Possibly however the knowledge of
his own soul-languor made him admire Shakespeare's strength ; and when the English Titan
thrusts forth Pelion on Ossa in his passionate
scenes, scaling the very skies, this poor critic
drops his pen in amazement sighing and whimpering in silence. As a pietist he ought actually
to hate that poet whose soul is steeped in the
blooming bliss of the gods, and whose every
word breathes forth the happiest paganism.
He ought to hate this believer in the creed of
life, who, while turning away in secret from the
creed of death and delighting in the sweet
tremors of ancient heroism, refuses to have
aught to do with renunciation and hypocrisy !
But notwithstanding he loves him, and in his
untiring love he would like to convert Shakespeare to the true church. He reasons Shakespeare into a Christian frame of mind; by pious
make-believe or by self-deception he discovers
this *Christian frame of mind* in all Shake-

speare's Plays and the holy water of his expositions forms, as it were, a five-volumed
baptism with which he sprinkles this great
heathen's head.

But I repeat, these expositions are not quite
without genius. Sometimes Franz Horn gets
hold of a good idea; then he cuts all kinds
of tedious sour-sweet faces, groaning and turning himself over and over before the begetting
of a thought, and when at last he has seized
on a good idea, he smiles expectantly like a
weary simpleton. It is really as vexing as it
is absurd that Franz Horn, this weak-minded
pietist, has reviewed Shakespeare. In juxtaposition to this, Grabbe in one of his comedies
makes Shakespeare go to hell, where he has to
review the works of Franz Horn.[1]

The enthusiastic devotion with which clever
actors gave themselves up to the representation
of Shakespeare's Plays did more to bring them
before the public than the insincere praises,
expositions and tedious panegyrics of the critics.
In his English letters Lichtenberg gives us
some valuable information concerning the
masterly way in which Shakespeare's charac-

[1] "Jokes, Satire, Irony and Insinuations," a Comedy in
3 Acts. Dramatic Works of Grabbe. Vol. ii. N.B. Act ii.
Scene ii., p. 125.

ters were performed in England during the last century. I say his characters, not his works *in toto*, for to this day English actors have only noted that which is specially Shakespearian, not that which belongs to the universal domain of poetry or of art. In the case of Shakespeare's critics who, wearing spectacles dim from over-much study, cannot perceive the simplest, nearest, and most natural things, this narrow conception becomes yet narrower when applied to his plays. Garrick got a better hold of Shakespeare's thought than Dr. Johnson, the John Bull of erudition on whose nose Queen Mab must have skipped about queerly enough, whilst he was writing about the Midsummer Night's Dream. He certainly did not know why Shakespeare occasioned him more involuntary irritation and desire to sneeze than any other of the poets he criticised.

Garrick, calling the dead to life by a terrible exorcism, so that they performed their horrible, sanguinary, and absurd deeds in the sight of all spectators, shook the entire English nation, whilst Dr. Johnson dissected Shakespeare's characters like so many dead bodies, displaying thereby his greatest nonsense in Ciceronian English, as he swung himself in awkward self-satisfied style on the antithesis of his Latin periods. But Garrick loved the great poet, and as a reward for such devotion he lies buried in Westminster Abbey, near the foot of Shakespeare's statue, like a faithful dog at his master's feet.

We owe the introduction of Garrick's method of acting into Germany to the celebrated Schroeder, who was the first to arrange some of Shakespeare's best plays for the German stage. Schroeder, like Garrick, understood neither the poetic nor the artistic value of these plays, he only felt that they were true to nature, and he sought less for the blessed harmony and the inner perfection of a play than to reproduce the single characters, as faithfully as it lay within the bounds of a limited nature so to do. This assertion is permissible, as we have accounts of his acting which are still considered of value on the Hamburg stage, as well as Shakespeare's plays arranged by him. These are utterly wanting in poetry and artistic arrangement, but they contain a certain easy naturalness, owing to a fusion of the most striking characteristics, and a firm delineation of the most important characters.

It was this system of naturalness which produced the great actor Devrient, whom I once saw at Berlin with Wolf, who followed the rules of art more closely than the former. Though these two started from quite different points of view, the one following nature, the other art, as the highest good, they met in the domain of poetry, and by means of their opposite methods overwhelmed and delighted the spectators.

The muses of music and painting have done less for Shakespeare than might have been supposed. Were they jealous of their sisters Melpomene and Thalia, whom the great Englishman had crowned with immortal laurels? No great composer has been grandly inspired by any Shakespearian play except by *Romeo and Juliet* and *Othello*. It is as little necessary to praise those sweet-sounding notes which came from the heart of Zingarelli, throbbing like that of a joyful nightingale, as it is to admire the sweet tones in which Pesaro's swan sings of tender Desdemona's bleeding wounds and the dark passions of her beloved. Painting, as all the pictorial arts, has done still less in praise of our poet. The so-called Shakespeare collection in Pall Mall shows the good intention, but the vapid weakness of English painters. They are insipid representations in the style of the older French paintings, without the good taste which these contain. Englishmen bungle as miserably in painting as they do in music. They are only admirable in portrait painting, and when they can use the engraver's style and lay aside the pallet they surpass all other European artists. Whence comes it that Englishmen, who have so poor a sense of colour, are such great designers, producing masterpieces in copper and steel engraving? We can see this in the subjoined portraits of women old and young, taken from the Plays of Shakespeare, the excellence of which is manifest. In fact, I do not criticise. This preface to the charming work was only meant as a slight bow, such as it is customary to give on a first introduction. I am the doorkeeper, opening the picture gallery, and so far you have heard only the jingling of the keys. I shall often, in taking you round, interrupt your contemplations by some cursory remark. Sometimes I shall follow the example of those *Cicerones* who never allow too much enthusiastic gazing at a picture, with a trifling remark they can disturb our contemplative rapture.

At any rate I think friends at home will be pleased with this publication. The sight of these lovely women's portraits may banish from their faces those marks of sadness, for which they have so much cause. Why cannot I offer you something more tangible than these beauti-

ful shadows? Why cannot I open for you the
portals of rosy reality? Once I thought of
breaking the halberds with which they guarded
the gardens of delight . . . but my strength
failed me, the halberdiers laughed, striking me
with their spears, and my bold and generous
heart was struck dumb with shame if not with
fear. Do I hear you sigh?

TRAGEDIES

CRESSIDA   [*Troilus and Cressida*]

I BEGIN by introducing the staid daughter of
Calchas to the honourable public. Pandarus,
a brave go-between whose officiousness was
almost superfluous, was her uncle. Troilus, a
son of the prolific Priam, was her first lover;
she went through all the formalities, pledged
him her troth, broke her word with due
decorum, and held a sorrowful monologue over
the weakness of a woman's heart, before she
yielded to Diomede. She is spoken of as
a strumpet by Thersites the eavesdropper,
who is rude enough always to call things by
their names. But possibly he will ultimately
have to use gentler language, for this beautiful
woman may yet fall to his share as a sweet
mistress, passing on from one less worthy hero
to another.

I had my reasons for commencing this collection of pictures by Cressida's portrait. I did

not give her the precedence of so many of Shakespeare's grandly ideal creations on account of her virtue, or because she *is* a type of the generosity of women. The portrait of this questionable lady comes first because in editing the complete works of Shakespeare I should always allow *Troilus and Cressida* to precede the rest. I do not know why Stevens, in his fine edition of Shakespeare's works, does the same; but I question whether the motive of this English editor was similar to mine.

Troilus and Cressida is the only play in which Shakespeare introduces those same heroes chosen by Greek poets as the *dramatis personæ* of their plays. Thus, while comparing these with the same characters described by the older poets, we get an insight into Shakespeare's method. Whilst the classic Greek poets seek to glorify reality, rising into idealism, our modern tragic poet peers more into the depths of things ; he discovers the hidden roots of appearances by the keen edge of his spirit, laying bare before our eyes the silent soil wherein they repose. The ancient writers of tragedy, like the sculptors of old, strove after beauty and nobility, glorifying the form rather than that which the form contained, but

Shakespeare aimed at truth and the underlying matter. He is thus a master in character-painting, which often causes him to verge on awkward caricature, whereby he divests the heroes of their bright armour and brings them before us in absurdly homely gear. Those writers who criticised *Troilus and Cressida* according to the rules drawn by Aristotle from the best Greek plays, must often have been in an awkward position, and apt to make ridiculous blunders. As a tragedy the play did not appear to them sufficiently earnest and pathetic, and all came to pass about as naturally as it does with us. The heroes behaved as foolishly and perhaps as barbarously as they do now, the hero in chief is a lout, and the heroine a common wench, of which we have examples enough among our near acquaintances . . . and even the most honoured names, celebrities of the heroic ages, such as the great Pelius Achilles, brave son of Thetis, what miserable appearances do they present. On the other hand the play could hardly rank as a comedy, for it teems with life, and there is a grand air about the wise speeches, as we perceive in the meditations of Ulysses, where he dwells on the necessity of authority, and which to this day merit close attention.

No, said the critics, a play in which such speeches are delivered cannot be a comedy, and still less could they believe that a poor rogue like the gymnast Massmann, with his small knowledge of Latin and Greek, could be so bold as to make use of these celebrated heroes of the classics, in a comedy!

No, *Troilus and Cressida* is neither a comedy nor a tragedy in the usual sense ; this play belongs to no special kind of fiction, and still less can it be judged by any received standard ; it is thoroughly Shakespearian. We can only testify to its general excellence ; were we to criticise it individually, we should need the help of that new æsthetic science which has yet to be written.

By registering this play as a tragedy, I would show from the commencement of what importance I consider these titles. My old poetry-master in the school at Düsseldorff once wittily remarked : "those plays which breathe forth the melancholy spirit of Melpomene instead of Thalia's happy spirit, belong to the domain of tragedy." Perhaps I was thinking of this when I placed *Troilus and Cressida* among the tragedies. And in truth it is pervaded by a gleeful bitterness, a withering irony such as we never find in the plays of the comic

muse. Rather is the muse of tragedy everywhere perceptible in this play, and her merriment and her jokes are a pretence. . . . We
seem to look on, whilst Melpomene dances the
cancan at a ball of *grisettes*, with shameless
laughter flitting across her pallid lips, and with
death in her heart.

CASSANDRA   [*Troilus and Cressida*]

HERE we have the soothsaying daughter of
Priam. She is endowed with that terrible
knowledge of the future, she proclaims the fall
of Troy and calls upon the gods, whilst Hector
arms himself for the fight with terrible Achilles.
. . . She can already see in her mind's eye
her beloved brother dying of his open wounds.
. . . In vain she calls upon the gods, no one
hears, and she sinks into the abyss of a gloomy
fate, as hopelessly lost as her whole blinded
nation.

Shakespeare's beautiful seer only utters a
few unimportant words; to him she is but an
ordinary prophet of evil running through the
cursed town with her cry of woe. We see her
according to the picture;

> " With eyes aflame, and
> Hair cast to the winds."

Our great Schiller has given a more lovely picture of her in one of his most beautiful poems. Here she reproaches the Pythian divinity for the misfortune he has brought upon his priestess, in piercing tones of sorrow. . . . I once had to recite this poem at a public examination at school, and stuck fast at the words :

> "When in sight of coming terror,
> Let us keep our shell'ring guise,
> While we live we're doomed to error,
> Only death can make us wise."

HELEN   [*Troilus and Cressida*]

THIS is beautiful Helen whose story I cannot entirely relate and explain, or I should have to commence with Leda's egg.

Tyndarus was her so-called father, but her secret progenitor was a god who according to a frequent ancient custom assumed the shape of a bird, and blessed her mother with a child. She married early and went to reside at Sparta, but we cannot wonder that her beauty caused her to elope from there, making a cuckold of king Menelaus her husband.

Let any fair lady who feels herself perfectly pure cast the first stone at her poor sister. By this, I do not mean to say that there are no

perfectly faithful women. Even the celebrated
Eve, the first of her sex, was a pattern of
marital fidelity. As she walked hand in hand
with her husband, who was clad in his apron of
fig-leaves, that world-famed Adam—then the
only man living—not the remotest thought of
adultery crossed her heart. She only liked to
converse with the serpent and this on account
of the fine French language which she acquired
by this means, being fond of improving her
mind. Oh! ye daughters of Eve, your first
mother set you an excellent example! . . .

Mother Venus, the immortal goddess of delight, procured the favour of beautiful Helen
for prince Paris. He broke the holy bonds of
hospitality and fled to Troy, that safe citadel,
with his beautiful prey. . . . We should all
have done the same under similar circumstances
and in particular we Germans, as we are more
learned than other nations and have busied
ourselves from youth upwards with Homer's
poems. Beautiful Helen is our first love, and
even as boys sitting on our forms at school,
while our master explained to us those beautiful Greek verses in which the aged Trojans
could not contain their delight at the sight of
Helen . . . even then sweet feelings of delight surged up wildly in our young inexperi-

enced hearts . . . and with blushing cheeks
and stammering lips we answered our master's
questions on grammar. . . . Later on, when
we grew older and rather learned, turning into
necromancers able to conjure up the devil, then
we demanded beautiful Helen of Sparta at the
hands of this faithful spirit. I have said on a
former occasion that in Johannes Faustus we
have a true example of the German nation, that
nation which in order to satiate its longing
thinks more of learning than of life. Though
this celebrated doctor, the typical German, ultimately thirsts after the enjoyment of the senses,
he by no means seeks the object of his choice
in the blooming fields of reality, but among
mildewy and learned books. And whilst a
French or Italian necromancer would have desired the most beautiful woman of present times
at the hands of Mephistopheles, the German
Faust desires a woman who has already been
dead a thousand years, and who smiles on him
like a beautiful shadow from ancient Greek
parchments. Helen of Sparta! This desire
is a very significant characteristic of the German nation.

Shakespeare has not given more attention to
beautiful Helen than to Cassandra in this play
of *Troilus and Cressida*. She appears on the

scenes with Paris and we hear her joking merrily with Pandarus the ancient go-between. She banters him and then desires him to sing a love-song with his bleating old voice. But occasionally a painful shadow of fear and pre-sentiment of a terrible catastrophe overcloud her lightheartedness. From jokes sweet as roses, serpents stretch forth their tiny black heads, and she betrays the tenor of her mind in the words,

"Let thy song be love: this love will undo us all. Oh, Cupid, Cupid, Cupid!"

VIRGILIA [*Coriolanus*]

HERE is the wife of Coriolanus, a shy dove who does not even venture to coo in the presence of her haughty husband. She looks down modestly when he returns victorious from the fight and all rush forward to greet him, and the smiling hero calls her very significantly; "my gracious Silence"! This silence is the key to her whole character, she is silent as the blushing rose, as the chaste pearl, as the evening star in its longing, as the heart of man in its delight . . . hers is a perfect, rare, passionate silence, more expressive than eloquence or than any rhetorical bombast. She is a shy, tender woman, and presents in her soft loveliness a striking contrast to her mother-in-law Volumnia, the Roman she-wolf, who had once suckled the wolf Caius Marcius with her iron milk. Indeed Volumnia is a true matron, and her young brood sucked in nought but wild courage, rebellious defiance, and scorn of the people, from her patrician breasts.

In the tragedy of *Coriolanus* Shakespeare produces for us a hero who, having imbibed virtues and vices at an early age, has gained the laurel-crown of celebrity by foregoing the nobler oak-crown of good fellowship. This brings him to a miserable end, inasmuch as he commits a terrible crime and betrays his country.

From *Troilus and Cressida* where the poet borrows his materials from the heroic times of ancient Greece, I turn to Coriolanus in which we can perceive the manner in which he handles Roman events. He here describes the disputes between Patricians and Plebeians in ancient Rome.

I do not maintain that he has kept exactly to the facts of Roman history in the play before us ; but the poet has most thoroughly represented and entered into the spirit of these disputes. As there are many events at this present day which bear a resemblance to those sad quarrels which the privileged Patricians and degraded Plebeians formerly waged with one another, we are better able to judge of this. Shakespeare might be a poet of the present day living in London, and describing the Radicals and Tories of the present time under a Roman mask. We are borne out in this opinion by the great resemblance which exists between ancient Romans and modern Englishmen, as also between their respective statesmen. Indeed a certain prosaic hardness, avarice, bloodthirstiness, untiring energy and firmness of character, is as peculiar to the Englishman of this as it was to the Roman of a former age; only that the latter bore more resemblance to a land rat than to a water rat. They resemble each other in their want of amiability, which each carries to the highest point. The greatest affinity exists between the aristocracy of either nation. The English nobleman, like the Roman aristocrat of ancient times, is patriotic; his patriotism forms a link of intimacy with the people in spite of divergent political rights, and the result is a complete and united nation of aristocrats and democrats, similar to that which existed in ancient Rome. This is not the case in other countries, where the nobility are less tied to the soil, and where they depend more on the favour of the reigning prince, or where they devote themselves exclusively to the private interests of their own class. Again, the English nobility resemble the Roman, in considering authority the highest, most praiseworthy, and really most lucrative thing to strive after. I say most lucrative, as the highest offices of state are controlled by abused favouritism and customary extortion in the England of to-day as in the Rome of old, which means that these positions are bought and sold. The English like the Roman aristocracy, make these positions the aim of a young man's education, and with both, the arts of war and debate are reckoned among the best means for procuring future authority. The tradition of good governing capacities is maintained among English families of rank, as it was formerly at Rome ; and thus the English Tories will probably remain as indispensable and as long in power, as did the senatorial families of ancient Rome.

But nothing so resembles the present condition of England, as the canvassing for votes, described in *Coriolanus*. With what inward rage and scornful irony do we see the Roman Tory canvassing for the votes of those good citizens whom he despises from the bottom of his heart, but whose votes are indispensable if he is to be elected consul. Only the majority of English lords having earned their scars rather in fox-hunting than in battle, and having learned the art of dissimulation from their mothers, do not now evince such rage and scorn at parliamentary elections, as did the obstinate Coriolanus.

As ever, Shakespeare shows the greatest impartiality in this play. The aristocrat is right in despising his plebeian voters, for he feels that he behaved more bravely in battle, which the Romans regarded as the greatest virtue. But on the other hand, the poor voters, the people, are also right in opposing him in spite of this virtue; for he made them understand sufficiently clearly that he would cease to distribute bread in his position of consul,—"but bread is the nation's first right."

PORTIA [*Julius Cæsar*]

Cæsar's popularity was chiefly based on his liberality and his generosity towards the people. In him the nation recognised the founder of those better times which awaited it in his descendants the emperors, for they allowed the people to enjoy their first right; they gave them their daily bread. Those cruel and arbitrary acts of which the emperors were guilty towards several hundred patrician families, by which their privileges were laughed to scorn, we gladly pardon ; we gratefully recognise in the emperors, the destroyers of that *régime* of nobles, who allow the people the lowest wages for the hardest service ; we honour in them human saviours who introduced civil equality by abasing the great and exalting the lowly. Let patrician Tacitus, that advocate of the past, describe in his poetical and venomous phraseology the sins and madnesses of the Cæsars ; we know something better of them—they fed the people.

Cæsar prepares the fall of the Roman aristocracy, and the victory of democracy. Meanwhile many old patricians are imbued with a spirit of republicanism, they cannot yet bear to see the chief power centred in one person— they cannot live where one individual dares to carry his head higher than they do, though it be the magnificent head of a Julius Cæsar, and they sharpen their daggers and kill him.

It is wrongly asserted at the present day that democracy and monarchy are opposed to one another. The ideal democracy is that in which an individual heads the state, representing thus the popular will incarnate, even as God rules the world. Men obtain their safest equality,

the most perfect form of democracy, when
governed by this incarnation of the popular
will, representative of God in His Majesty. So
also aristocracy and republicanism are not
inimical to one another, and this is clearly
shown in the play before us, where the spirit
of republicanism becomes most evident in the
haughtiest aristocrats. In the case of Cassius
these characteristics are more marked than in
Brutus. Long ago we remarked that a certain
narrow jealousy enduring nothing over it,
fosters the republican spirit. It is a petty spirit
of envy which hates everything that soars aloft
and which cannot even bear to see virtue personified, fearing that a virtuous man may assert
his greater individuality too strongly. The
republicans of the present day may therefore
be likened to deists, whose supreme ambition
is modesty—they like to imagine that men are
but miserable figures modelled in clay, who
having been fashioned after one image in the
hands of one creator, are bound to abstain from
all proud love of distinction or ambitious pomp.
In puritanism the English republicans once
hailed a similar principle, and this may also be
said of the republicans of ancient Rome,—they
were in fact stoics. Bearing this in mind the
sagacity with which Shakespeare has described

Cassius is admirable, especially when he is made to converse with Brutus, whilst he hears the people welcoming Cæsar with cries of delight, whom they wish to elect as king.

> " I cannot tell what you and other men
> Think of this life; but for my single self,
> I had as lief not be as live to be
> In awe of such a thing as I myself.
> I was born free as Cæsar; so were you :
> We both have fed as well; and we can both
> Endure the winter's cold as well as he :
> For once, upon a raw and gusty day,
> The troubled Tiber chafing with her shores,
> Cæsar said to me, ' Dar'st thou, Cassius, now
> Leap in with me into the angry flood,
> And swim to yonder point?' Upon the word,
> Accoutred as I was, I plungéd in
> And bade him follow : so indeed he did.
> The torrent roared ; and we did buffet it
> With lusty sinews, throwing it aside
> And stemming it with hearts of controversy :
> But ere we could arrive the point proposed
> Cæsar cried, 'Help me, Cassius, or I sink !'
> I, as Æneas our great ancestor
> Did from the flames of Troy upon his shoulder
> The old Anchises bear, so from the waves of Tiber
> Did I the tirèd Cæsar, and this man
> Is now become a god ; and Cassius is
> A wretched creature and must bend his body
> If Cæsar carelessly but nod on him.
> He had a fever when he was in Spain,
> And when the fit was on him, I did mark,
> How he did shake : 'tis true, this god did shake.

His coward lips did from their colour fly;
And that same eye, whose bend doth awe the world
Did lose his lustre: I did hear him groan,
Ay, and that tongue of his that bade the Romans
Mark him, and write his speeches in their books,
Alas it cried, ' Give me some drink, Titinius '
As a sick girl.   Ye gods, it doth amaze me
A man of such a feeble temper should
So get the start of the majestic world,
And bear the palm alone."

Cæsar himself sees through Cassius perfectly,
and his words to Antony are very expressive.

" Let me have men about me that are fat;
Sleek-headed men, and such as sleep o' nights:
Yond' Cassius has a lean and hungry look;
He thinks too much : such men are dangerous.

.   .   .   .   .

Would he were fatter!—but I fear him not;
Yet if my name were liable to fear,
I do not know the man I should avoid
So soon as that spare Cassius.   He reads much;
He is a great observer and he looks
Quite thro' the deeds of men : he loves no plays
As thou dost, Antony; he hears no music:
Seldom he smiles, and smiles in such a sort
As if he mocked himself and scorned his spirit
That could be moved to smile at anything.
Such men as he be never at heart's ease
Whiles they behold a greater than themselves !
And therefore are they very dangerous."

Cassius is a republican, and as we often find

with such men, he prefers the friendship of noble men to the love of tender women. On the other hand Brutus sacrifices himself to the republic, not because he is a republican by nature, but because virtue is his sole desire, and he regards that sacrifice as the highest duty. He is open to all soft feelings and loves Portia his wife, with tender affection.

Portia, a daughter of Cato, is Roman in her character, but nevertheless she is lovable, and manifests in her highest flights of heroism womanly feeling and thoughtful womanliness. With anxious love she observes every shadow that crosses her husband's brow, betraying his troubled thoughts. She will know what troubles him, with him she will share the secret that weighs down his spirit . . . And when at last she does know it, she remains a woman, almost dies of the terrible anxiety which she cannot conceal and acknowledges :

> "I have a man's mind, but a woman's might.
> How hard it is for women to keep counsel!"

CLEOPATRA   [*Antony and Cleopatra*]

Now behold the celebrated Queen of Egypt who ruined Antony.

He knows that this woman is goading him

on to ruin and wishes to tear himself away from her magic influence. . . .

> "I must with haste from hence."

He flies . . . but only in order to return the more quickly to the flesh-pots of Egypt and to his "Serpent of Old Nile" as he calls her . . . soon he is with her again sweltering in splendid Alexandrian mud, and there Octavius relates:

> "I' the market-place on a tribunal silvered
> Cleopatra and himself in chairs of gold
> Were publicly enthroned; at the feet sat
> Cæsarion, whom they call my father's son,
> And all th' unlawful issue that their lust
> Since then hath made between them.   Unto her
> He gave the establishment of Egypt; made her
> Of lower Syria, Cyprus, Lydia,
> Absolute queen.
>
>   .   .   .   .   .
>
> I' the common show-place where they exercise
> His sons he there proclaimed the kings of kings;
> Great Media, Parthia and Armenia,
> He gave to Alexander; to Ptolemy he assigned
> Syria, Cilicia and Phoenicia: she
> In the habiliments of the goddess Isis
> That day appeared; and oft before gave audience
> As 'tis reported, so."

The Egyptian sorceress takes possession of his head as well as of his heart, and makes havoc of his talent as a great general. Instead of waging war on *terra firma* where victory has always been his, he gives battle on the uncertain ocean where his courage is of less account; and thence where this fanciful woman was bent on following him, she suddenly takes to flight with all her vessels, just in the decisive moment of battle, and Antony, "like an amorous drake," pursues her with flying sails, leaving honour and good fortune behind. But the unhappy hero does not suffer his worst defeat owing to Cleopatra's weak-minded fancies alone; later on she treacherously betrays him, and in secret league with Octavius allows her fleet to go over to the enemy. . . . In order to save her own goods in the shipwreck of his happiness, or may be to procure for herself yet greater advantages, she deceives him in the meanest way. She drives him to despair and death by her cunning and hypocrisy . . . and still he loves her devotedly to the end; indeed his love is only the more inflamed after her betrayal of him. He certainly curses her constant artfulness, he knows her faults and in most brutal language betrays his better discernment, telling her the bitterest truths.

"You were half blasted ere I knew you:—ha!
Have I my pillow left unpressed in Rome

Forborne the getting of a lawful race
And by a gem of women, to be abused
By one that looks on feeders?

.   .   .   .

You have been a boggler ever :
But when we in our viciousness grow hard—
Oh misery on't !—the wise gods seal our eyes ;
In our own filth drop our clear judgments ; make us
Adore our errors ; laugh at 's while we strut
To our confusion.

.   .   .   .   .

I found you as a morsel cold upon
Dead Cæsar's trencher ; nay, you were a fragment
Of Cneius Pompey's ; besides what hotter hours
Unregistered in vulgar fame, you have
Luxuriously picked out."

But just as the spear of Achilles could heal
the wounds which it had made, so could this
lover's lips heal by an embrace the mortal
wounds with which his sharp words had pierced
the soul of his beloved, . . . and after every
evil action to which this old Serpent of the Nile
treated the Roman Wolf, and after every howling invective in which the latter indulged in
consequence, the more tenderly did these two
embrace. Even in dying we find him press-
ing on her lips the last kiss of so many
kisses. . . .

But she also, the Egyptian Serpent, how she
loves her Roman Wolf! Her treacheries are

only the external turns and twists of an evil serpent-nature ; she practises them mechanic-ally from an inborn or habitual proneness to transgress . . . but in the depths of her being she retains the most unchanging love towards Antony ; she is not herself aware that this love is so strong, often she thinks it may be conquered or trifled with. But she errs, and she clearly recognises her error at the moment of losing her beloved for ever, when her sorrow bursts forth in the fine words :

"I dreamed there was an emperor Antony :
Oh such another sleep that I might see
But such another man.

.   .   .   .   .

His face was as the heavens ; and therein stuck
A sun and moon, which kept their course and lighted
The little O, the earth.

.   .   .   .   .

His legs bestrid the ocean : his reared arm
Crested the world ; his voice was propertied
As all the tunèd spheres, and that to friends ;
But when he meant to quail and shake the orb,
He was as rattling thunder. For his bounty
There was no winter in't ; an autumn 'twas
That grew the more by reaping : his delights
Were dolphin-like ; they showed his back above
The element they lived in : in his livery
Walked crowns and crownets ; realms and islands were
As plates dropped from his pocket."

This Cleopatra is a woman. She loves and betrays at the same time. We err in thinking that women cease to love us when they betray us. They do but follow their nature ; and even if they have no desire to empty the forbidden cup to the dregs, they would often like to take a sip, just to touch the cup's edge with their lips at least, in order to taste what poison is like. Besides Shakespeare, no one has treated this phenomenon in the play before us so well as the old Abbé Prévost in his novel ; *Manon Lescaut*. Here there is a resemblance between the intuition of the greatest poet and the calm observation of the coolest prosaist.

Yes, this Cleopatra is a woman in the most lovely and the most cursed sense. She reminds me of Lessing's words ; " when God created woman, he took too fine a clay." The delicacy of such material can only seldom meet life's demands. Such beings are too good and too bad for this world. With them the sweetest virtues are the cause of the worst sins. When Cleopatra first comes upon the scene, Shakespeare paints the brightly capricious spirit by which the beautiful queen is always possessed, in delightfully true colours. This often shows itself in most doubtful questions and desires, and may possibly be regarded as the final cause of all her actions. Nothing is more characteristic than the fifth scene of the first act where she desires her attendant to give her a sleeping draught of mandrake, in order to while away the time of Antony's absence. Then the devil possesses her to call her eunuch, Mardian. He asks submissively what his mistress wants of him. She answers:

"not now to hear thee sing; I take no pleasure
in aught an eunuch has:—hast thou affections?"

Mardian

Yes, gracious Madam.

Cleopatra

Indeed!

Mardian

Not in deed, Madam; for I can do nothing
But what indeed is honest to be done:
Yet have I fierce affections and I think
What Venus did with Mars.

Cleopatra

Oh, Charmian
Where think'st thou he is now? Stands he or sits he?
Or does he walk? Or is he on his horse?
Oh, happy horse to bear the weight of Antony!
Do bravely, horse! for wott'st thou whom thou mov'st?
The demi-Atlas of this earth, the arm
And burgonet of men. He's speaking now
Or murmuring, 'Where's my Serpent of Old Nile?'
For so he calls me."

Were I to express all I think regardless of
malicious smiles, I should have to declare my
conviction that this flighty feeling and thinking
of Cleopatra, which is a sequence of a flighty,
idle and unquiet life, bears resemblance to the
acts of a certain class of extravagant women.
Their expensive housekeeping is not always
supplied by conjugal generosity ; often they
vex and gladden the hearts of their titular
husbands with love and devotion, often with
simple love, and always with mad fancies. And
this Cleopatra, who could never have defrayed
her unheard of luxury from the crown revenues
of Egypt, and who received from her Roman
lover Antony the extorted treasure of whole
provinces as a gift, being in the truest sense
a maintained queen—was this Cleopatra really
anything else ?

From this character of Cleopatra, so excitable,
flighty, so made up of extremes and sultry in its
passion, there flashes forth an element of sen-
sual, wild, and sulphurous wit, which frightens
more than it delights. Plutarch gives us an
idea of this comic element, displaying itself
rather in acts than in words, and even at school
I laughed heartily at this mystified Antony,
who went out fishing with his royal mistress
only to hook salted fish. For in secret the sly

Egyptian woman had ordered a number of
divers hidden under the water to fasten a salted
fish on to the hook of this amorous Roman
each time he sent down his line. Our master
looked very solemn over this anecdote and
severely blamed the wicked wantonness with
which the queen treated the lives of her subjects, those poor divers, for the sake of a joke.
Altogether our master disapproved of Cleopatra,
and he seriously drew our attention to the
fact that owing to this woman Antony spoiled
his entire career as a statesman, becoming
entangled in domestic difficulties and ending
miserably.

Yes, my old master was right; it is very
dangerous to come in too close contact with
a person like Cleopatra. A hero may come to
grief thereby, but only a hero. Here as everywhere else steady-going mediocrity is in no
danger.

Cleopatra's position and character have in
them decidedly comic elements. This capricious, pleasure-loving, fickle, feverish coquette,
this ancient *parisienne*, this goddess of life
flutters and rules over Egypt, the silent petri-
fied land of the dead . . . You know it
well that Egypt, that mysterious Mizraim with
its narrow Nile valley, in appearance like a

coffin . . . In the high reeds the crocodile or the hidden child of Holy Writ is shedding its tears . . . We see temples with co-lossal pillars against which hideous forms of sacred animals recline, painted in ugly gaudy colours . . . At the doorway the monk of Isis with his hieroglyphical hood nods to us. . . . Mummies hold their siesta in luxurious villas and their gilded mask keeps them from the fly-swarms of decay . . . There stand the narrow obelisks and wide pyramids like dumb thoughts . . . The Moon mountains of Œthiopia hiding the sources of the Nile nod to us in the back-ground. . . . Every-where we behold death, stone and mystery. . . . And over this land beautiful Cleopatra reigned as queen.

Great is the wit of God! *Shakespeare !*

LAVINIA   [*Titus Andronicus*]

In Julius Cæsar we see the last throes of the republican spirit struggling vainly against ap-proaching monarchism. The republic has out-lived itself. Brutus and Cassius can only murder the man who first attempted to grasp a royal crown; they cannot kill monarchism, which is deeply rooted in the needs of the time. Instead of one fallen Cæsar we get in the play

of *Antony and Cleopatra* three other Cæsars
who boldly attempt to seize the dominion of the
world. As a principle the question has been
solved, and the war waged between these Tri-
umvirs becomes a personal one. Who shall be
emperor and master over all men and nations?
In the tragedy of *Titus Andronicus* we perceive
how the unlimited power of one individual
follows in the Roman empire the law of all
terrestrial things, and that it is doomed to decay. Nothing is more despicable than the sight
of these later Cæsars, who added hollow weakness to the madness and the crimes of their
Neros and Caligulas. These Neros and Caligulas lost their head when at the height of
their power; thinking themselves more than
men, they became inhuman; thinking themselves gods, they became godless; we can
hardly in our amazement judge of them by
ordinary standards on account of their enor-
mities. The later Cæsars on the other hand
are rather objects of compassion, dislike and
horror. They lack that heathen self-adoration,
that intoxication of solitary majesty, and that
terrible irresponsibility . . . Like good
christians they are crushed in spirit, the black-
cowled confessor has spoken to them seriously,
and they have come to regard themselves as

poor worms depending on the mercy of a more divine majesty with the prospect of some day being tortured and roasted in hell on account of their earthly sins.

Though the play of *Titus Andronicus* bears the outer garb of heathenism, it has the character of a later christian time and the moral perversion of all ethical and social things is thoroughly Byzantine in tone. This play must certainly be reckoned among Shakespeare's earliest works, though many of his critics dispute its authenticity. It contains a pitilessness, a pronounced love of the hideous, a titanic struggle with the divine powers such as we often find in the early works of the greatest poets. The hero is a true Roman, a remnant of the old fossil age, in contradistinction to his demoralised surroundings. Did such men then still exist ? Possibly ; for as we find on the mountain-tops, nature loves to preserve some one example of any type which is about to disappear or to undergo transformation, be it even as a fossil. Titus Andronicus is such a fossilised Roman, and his fossil-like virtue is extremely curious, occurring as it does at the time of the later Cæsars.

The description of the violation and mutilation of his daughter Lavinia are among the

most terrible scenes to be found in any author.
The story of Philomela in Ovid's Metamor-
phoses is not nearly as ghastly, for the poor
Roman woman has her hands chopped off in
order not to betray the authors of this most
horrible deed. The father by his inflexible
manliness, the daughter by her noble womanliness, both point to a more moral past. She
fears dishonour not death, and very touching
are the chaste words in which she entreats the
empress Tamora, her enemy, for mercy, just as
the empress's sons are about to dishonour her :

> " 'Tis present death I beg ; and one thing more
> That womanhood denies my tongue to tell :
> Oh, keep me from their worse than killing lust,
> And tumble me into some loathsome pit,
> Where never man's eye may behold my body,
> Do this and be a charitable murderer."

In her maidenly purity Lavinia forms a perfect contrast to the forenamed empress Tamora;
here, as in most of his plays, Shakespeare places
two women of entirely different mould next to
one another, in order that we may read their
characters by the force of contrast. We had an
example of this in *Antony and Cleopatra* where
the dark, vain, licentious, voluptuous Egyptian
woman stands out in strong contrast to the

white, cold, moral, intensely prosaic and homely Octavia.

But Tamora also is a fine creature, and I think it somewhat unjust in the English engraver not to have included her in this collection of Shakespeare's women. She is a beautiful, majestic woman, a bewitching, imperial figure with the marks of a fallen divinity on her brow, and with an expression in her eyes which denotes consuming desire, one of magnificent wickedness thirsting after red blood. In the very first scene in which Tamora appears Shakespeare, owing to his far-seeing beneficence, appears to condone in advance the horrible acts of which she afterwards becomes guilty towards Titus Andronicus. For this stern Roman, untouched by her agonising maternal entreaties, permits her beloved son to be sacrificed before her very eyes. As soon as the young emperor begins to court her, by which hopes of future vengeance arise in her heart, she pronounces the gleefully ominous words :—

> " I'll let them know what 'tis to let a queen
> Kneel in the streets and beg for grace in vain."

Even as we excuse her cruelty on account of the over-abundance of misery she had to endure, so also the romantic poetry which is breathed forth in her words almost ennobles her execrably low behaviour in becoming the paramour of an odious Moor. Indeed that scene in which the Empress Tamora leaves her suite during the hunt in order to meet her beloved Moor in the forest, belongs to the weirdly sweet imagination of romantic poetry.

> " My lovely Aaron, wherefore look'st thou sad,
>   When everything doth make a gleeful boast?
>   The birds chant melody on every bush ;
>   The snake lies rollèd in the cheerful sun ;
>   The green leaves quiver with the cooling wind
>   And make a chequered shadow on the ground :
>   Under their sweet shade, Aaron, let us sit,
>   And whilst the babbling echo mocks the hounds,
>   Replying shrilly to the well-tuned horns,
>   As if a double hunt were heard at once,
>   Let us sit down and mark their yelping noise ;
>   And after conflict such as was supposed
>   The wandering prince and Dido once enjoyed,
>   And curtained with a counsel-keeping cave—
>   We may each wreathèd in the other's arms,
>   Our pastimes done, possess a golden slumber ;
>   Whiles hounds and horns and sweet melodious birds
>   Be unto us as is a nurse's song
>   Of lullaby to bring her babe asleep."

But whilst the eyes of the beautiful empress are lighted up with an expression of passionate longing, flickering bewitchingly like forked lightning over the Moor's dark form, he is thinking of far more important things, even the execution of most shameful intrigues, and his answer forms a harsh contrast to Tamora's fervent words.

CONSTANCE   [*King John*]

IT was on the 29th of August, A.D. 1827, that I gradually fell asleep over the first performance of a new tragedy by E. Raupach at the theatre at Berlin.

For those of the learned public who are no play-goers and only know standard literature I will observe, that the forenamed E. Raupach is a very useful man, a dealer in tragedies and comedies furnishing the Berlin stage with some new masterpiece from his collection every month. The theatre at Berlin is an excellent institution, and particularly useful for Hegelian philosophers who at night like to rest from their arduous day's labour of much thinking. The mind can there find a far more natural refreshment than at Wisotzkis. People go to the theatre, lean back lazily in their velvet stalls, peer at their neighbours through eye-glasses or at the legs of the ballet dancer just making her appearance, and if those actor-fellows do not scream too lustily, the spectators gently fall asleep as I did on the 29th of August, A.D. 1827.

When I awoke darkness surrounded me, and I could perceive by the faint glimmer of a lamp that I was by myself in the empty theatre. I was determined to spend the remainder of the night there and tried to fall asleep again. In this I was less successful than some hours previously when the opium fumes of Raupach's verses benumbed my brain. Besides this I was too much disturbed by the gnawing and singing of the mice. A whole colony of mice were audible near the orchestra, and I could not help overhearing their conversation, as I understand the language of all other animals besides Raupach's verses. Their talk was on subjects which must specially interest thoughtful people; on the final causes of all appearances, on the nature of things in themselves, on fate and freewill, on Raupach's great tragedy which had shortly before begun proceeded and ended with every imaginable horror before our very eyes.

"You young people," said an old mouse, "have only seen one or few such plays, but I am old and have seen many, observing them with careful attention. And I have found that their inherent qualities are all alike, that they are mostly only variations of the same theme, and that frequently they possess the very same expositions, complications and catastrophes. Always there are the same men and the same passions, merely changing costumes and figures of speech. There are the same incitements to action; love, hate, ambition, jealousy, whether the hero wear a Roman toga or ancient German armour, a turban or a felt hat, whether he behave in ancient or romantic fashion, simple or adorned, talking in bad iambics or worse trochaics. The whole history of man, which might be divided into various plays, acts and scenes remains ever the same; it is only a masked recurrence of the same characters and events, an organic circle ever beginning again from the beginning. And if *that* has once been taken to heart evil can no longer cause vexation, good can no longer cause special delight. We smile at the foolishness of those heroes who sacrifice themselves for the good and the happiness of the human race; we are amused whilst we remain wisely calm."

A chuckling voice, which appeared to belong to a small shrew-mouse, here hastily remarked; "I too have made my observations and not only from one standpoint, no troublesome jumps were too much for me. I left the platform and looked at things behind the scenes, and I there made many extraordinary discoveries. This hero whom you have just been admiring is no hero at all, for I heard a youngster call him a drunken wretch, giving him several kicks which he received without a word. That virtuous princess, who seemed to fall a sacrifice to her virtue, is neither a princess nor virtuous, for I saw her take red paint from a small china vase and *rouge* her cheeks, which gave her a modestly blushing appearance. At last she began to yawn and threw herself into the arms of a lieutenant of the guard, who promised her on his word of honour that she would find excellent herring-salad and a glass of punch in his room. What seemed to be thunder and lightning was only the trundling of some tin-roller and the blazing up of several ounces of resin. And even that stout, honest-looking citizen, with the unselfish and generous exterior, quarrelled avariciously with a lean man whom he called the manager of the theatre, and from whom he desired a few dollars increase in pay. Yes, I saw and heard all with my own eyes and ears; all the great and noble things here acted before us are mere deception; selfishness and egotism are the secret springs of all action, and wise people are not deceived by appearances."

But here arose a sad and whimpering voice apparently well known to me, though I could not tell whether it belonged to a male or female mouse. This mouse began by complaining of the frivolity of the times, lamented the infidelity and scepticism, and dwelt much on its capacity for loving. "I love you," it sighed forth, "and I tell you the truth. But truth was mercifully revealed to me in a holy hour. I also crept about endeavouring to discover the final causes of the chequered events which came to pass on the stage, endeavouring besides to find a few bread-crumbs in order to appease my bodily wants, for I love you. Suddenly I discovered a somewhat capacious hole or rather box, in in which sat a spare little man, clothed in grey, holding in his hand a roll of paper and repeating to himself in a monotonously low voice all the speeches which were being loudly and passionately uttered on the stage. A mystic shudder passed through my frame, in spite of my unworthiness I had the honour of being admitted into the holy of holies. I beheld myself in the presence of that mysterious primeval spirit, of the pure soul, by whose will terrestrial things are governed, by whose word they are created, and by whose fiat they can be made and unmade. For I noticed that those very heroes whom I had greatly admired just before, only seemed certain of their parts when they repeated his words in good faith, and that on the contrary they stammered and stumbled pitifully when they kept at a proud distance and did not hear his voice. I saw that every-thing was created by him ; he was the Almighty One in his holy box. On either side of it lamps shone brilliantly, flutes and violins sounded, light and music enveloped him, and he swam in harmonious rays of light and beaming har-monies."

But finally this speech became so nasal and whimpering that I could not understand much more of it, only occasionally I heard the words, " Preserve me from cats and traps, give me my daily crumbs. I love you for ever and ever ! Amen ! "

I relate this dream in order to express my opinion regarding the different philosophical standpoints from which the history of terres-trial things is generally viewed, thus at the same time informing people of my views and explaining why I do not burden these light pages with a real philosophy of English his-tory.

Indeed I have no desire dogmatically to explain the great events of English history which Shakespeare has glorified in his works ; I only desire to add a few ornamental words to those women's portraits which owe their origin to the poetical works of Shakespeare. As women play nothing less than the chief part in these historical plays, and as the poet never brings them on to the stage as he does in his other plays, with the purpose of describing the persons and characters of women, but rather because their co-operation is required in the history of which he treats, I also shall devote but a short space to them.

Constance comes first, looking very sorrowful. Like the Mater Dolorosa she bears her child on her arm.

> " Thy sins are visited in this poor child."

> .   .   .   .

> " All punish'd in the person of this child."

Madame Stich once performed the part of this sorrowing queen on the Berlin stage with great ability. That good Maria Louisa who at the time of the Invasion represented Queen Constance on the royal stage of France was less successful. However a certain Madame Caroline, who acted some years ago in the provinces, especially in Canton Vendée, did it execrably. She was not devoid of talent or of passion, but she was afflicted with *embonpoint*, which is a misfortune for an actress who desires to appear in the heroic part of a royal widow.

LADY PERCY   [*Henry IV.*]

IN this picture she is more plump and full-faced than I had imagined. But possibly the sharp features and slim waist which reveal themselves in her words and which give her spiritual physiognomy a certain stamp, are more interesting when contrasted with her well-rounded exterior. She is merry, hearty, and healthy in mind and body. Prince Henry would gladly disgust us with this lovely woman and parodies her and her Percy.

"I am not yet of Percy's mind the Hotspur of the North ; he that kills me some six or seven dozen of Scots at a breakfast, washes his hands and says to his wife, ' Fie upon this quiet life, I want work.' 'Oh, my sweet Harry,' says she, ' how many hast thou killed to-day ? ' ' Give my roan horse a drench,' says he, and answers ; ' Some fourteen,' an hour after—' a trifle, a trifle ! ' "

The scene in which we are introduced to Percy's home, and in which the blustering

hero's wife tames him with her boldest words
of affection is as charming as it is short ;

"Come, come, you paraquito, answer me
　　Directly unto this question that I ask :
　　In faith I'll break thy little finger, Harry,
　　An if thou wilt not tell me all things true.

Percy.

　　　　　　　　　　　　　　Away,
Away, you trifler !　Love ?　I love thee not,
I care not for thee, Kate ; this is no world
To play with mammets and to tilt with lips ;
We must have bloody noses and cracked crowns
And pass them current too.　Gods me, my horse !
What say'st thou, Kate ?　What would'st thou have with
　　me ?

Lady Percy.

Do you not love me, do you not indeed ?
Well do not then ; for since you love me not
I will not love myself.　Do you not love me ?
Nay tell me if you speak in jest or no ?

Percy.

Come wilt thou see me ride ?
And when I am o' horseback I will swear
I love thee infinitely.　But hark you, Kate ;
I must not have you henceforth question me
Whither I go, nor reason whereabout ;
Whither I must I must ; and to conclude
This evening I must leave you, gentle Kate.
I know you wise but yet no further wise
Than Harry Percy's wife ; constant you are ;

But yet a woman ; and for secrecy
No lady closer ; for I well believe
Thou wilt not utter what thou dost not know
And so far will I trust thee, gentle Kate."

PRINCESS KATHARINE [*Henry V.*]

WE wonder whether Shakespeare really wrote
that scene in which Princess Katharine takes
an English lesson ; and I question whether the
French forms of speech so pleasing to the
heart of John Bull, are actually Shakespeare's.
An English jargon would have had an equally
comic effect, particularly as by using Romance
words and constructions, a French turn may
be given to English without any loss of grammar. An English dramatist using only old
Saxon idioms and forms of speech could in like
manner give his writings a certain Germanic
turn. For English is made up of two hetero-
geneous elements ; the Romance and the Germanic. When jumbled together, these do not
form an organic whole ; they easily part company and then it is difficult to decide which of
them is legitimate English. We need only
compare the language used by Dr. Johnson or
Addison with that of Byron or Cobbett. Surely
Shakespeare had no need to make Princess
Katharine talk French.

I may here repeat what I have previously

stated, that Shakespeare is at fault in not making use of peculiar forms of speech in his historical plays, in order to draw a stronger contrast between the Norman-French character of the great nobles and the Anglo-Saxon character of the people. By doing this in his novels Walter Scott achieved his greatest success.

It was probably an Englishman's ill-will which caused the artist of the portrait before us to give this French princess rather a comical than a beautiful expression. She has the face of a bird, and her eyes look as though they belonged to some one else. Does she wear parrots' feathers on her head, and do they signify her powers of chattering? Her small white hands have an inquisitive look. She is made up of a vain love of display and a desire to please, and she knows how to play with her fan. I think her feet flirt with the very ground on which she treads.

JOAN OF ARC [*Henry VI. Part I.*]

HAIL to thee, great German Schiller, who hast not only freed yon grand figure from Voltaire's ugly sarcasm, but hast effaced from it the blot with which even Shakespeare invested it. . . . Indeed I do not know whether Shakespeare's

mind was imbued with an Englishman's anti-
pathy to the French, or whether it was ob-
scured by the superstition of the Middle Ages
when he represented this brave maiden as a
witch, in league with the dark powers of hell.
He describes her as calling upon the demons of
the lower regions, and regarded in this light
there is a reason for her cruel execution.
Every time I walk across the small market
place at Rouen where the maiden was burned
and where a miserable statue commemorates
this wicked deed, my anger breaks forth! To
kill by torture! Even then this was the manner in which the English behaved towards their
beaten foes! Next to the rock of St. Helena
this Rouen market place remains as a hateful
witness of English generosity!

Ah yes! Even Shakespeare is guilty of
injustice towards this noble maiden who saved
her country, and he treats her in an unfriendly
and unloving manner, even if he does not pro-
claim himself her decided enemy. And even
if she saved her country with the aid of hell,
she still deserves respect and admiration.

Or are the critics right, who hold that those
passages in which the maid makes her appearance, as also *Parts II. and III.* of *Henry
VI.* are not by Shakespeare? They maintain

that he only revised this trilogy which he took from older plays. I would gladly be of their opinion for the sake of the Maid of Orleans, but their arguments are untenable. In many parts these doubtful plays bear the full impress of Shakespeare's genius.

MARGARET   [*Henry VI. Part I.*]

HERE we see the beautiful daughter of Duke Regnier as a girl. Suffolk appears leading her prisoner, but before he is aware of it she has bewitched him. He reminds us of the recruit calling out to his captain from the sentry-box; "I have taken a prisoner,"—the captain replies,—"bring him to me then,"—the poor recruit answers; "I am unable to do so, for my prisoner will not let me go!"

Suffolk says:

"Be not offended, Nature's miracle,
   Thou art allotted to be ta'en by me:
   So doth the swan her downy cygnets save,
   Keeping them prisoners underneath her wings,
   Yet if this servile usage once offend,
   Go and be free again as Suffolk's friend.
            (*She turns away as if going.*)
   Oh stay! I have no power to let her pass;
   My hand would free her but my heart says no.
   As plays the sun upon the glassy streams,
   Twinkling another counterfeited beam
   So seems this gorgeous beauty to mine eyes.

Fain would I woo her, yet I dare not speak :
I'll call for pen and ink and write my mind:—
Lie de la Pole! disable not thyself;
Hast not a tongue? Is she not here thy prisoner?
Wilt thou be daunted at a woman's sight?
Ay, beauty's princely majesty is such,
Confounds the tongue and makes the senses crouch.

Margaret.

Say, Earl of Suffolk, if thy name be so—
What ransom must I pay before I pass?
For I perceive I am thy prisoner.

Suffolk (aside).

How canst thou tell she will deny thy suit
Before thou make a trial of her love?

Margaret.

Why speak'st thou not? What ransom must I pay?

Suffolk (aside).

She's beautiful and therefore to be wooed :
She is a woman, therefore to be won."

By marrying her to his king, thereby becoming her recognised subject and her secret lover, Suffolk finds he can retain her as his prisoner.

I do not know whether this *liaison* between Suffolk and Margaret is founded on fact. But Shakespeare possesses the seer's vision which can often perceive things not contained in chronicles, but which are nevertheless true. He can even remember those evanescent dreams of the past, which Clio forgot to note, possibly bright dreamy visions which do not disappear with actual events like common shadows, but which cling to the earth like spirits, and which are distinctly seen of those Sunday-born mortals, by us called Poets, whilst ordinary mortals of the work-day world go about their business unconcernedly, noting nothing of all this.

QUEEN MARGARET [*Hen. VI. Parts II. and III.*]

IN this picture we see the same Margaret as queen and wife of Henry VI. The bud has sprouted and we see the full-blown rose, but it contains a hideous canker. She is become a hard and wicked woman. Both in the actual and the fictitious world, the horror of that scene in which she hands the weeping duke of York a frightful kerchief steeped in his son's blood, mockingly advising him to dry his tears therewith, is unexampled. Terrible are the words :

> " Look, York, I stained this napkin with the blood
> That valiant Clifford with his rapier's point
> Made issue from the bosom of the boy ;
> And if thine eyes can water for his death
> I give thee this to dry thy cheeks withal.
> Alas, poor York ! but that I hate thee deadly,
> I should lament thy miserable state.

I prithee grieve to make me merry, York ;
Stamp, rave and fret that I may sing and dance."

Had beautiful Margaret's lips stood apart in this picture, we should have seen pointed teeth, like those of a carnivorous animal.

In the following play of *Richard III.*, she is become physically hideous, for she has lost her pointed teeth. She can no longer bite but only curse, and she murmurs forth slanders and curses as she wanders through the royal chambers, a spectral old woman with toothless mouth and evil tongue.

Shakespeare awakens in us a certain feeling of pity even for this unnatural woman on account of her love for wild Suffolk. We cannot deny the truth and fervour of her sinful passion. The farewell scene between the two lovers is very beautiful, and there is great tenderness in Margaret's words ;

" Go, speak not to me ; even now be gone—
Oh go not yet ! Even thus two friends condemned
Embrace and kiss and take ten thousand leaves
Lother a hundred times to part than die.
Yet now farewell, and farewell life with thee."

And Suffolk answers ;

" 'Tis not the land I care for, wert thou hence ;
A wilderness is populous enough,

So Suffolk had thy heavenly company :
For where thou art, there is the world itself
With every several pleasure in the world ;
And where thou art not, desolation."

When afterwards Margaret cries out in her
deep despair, as she bears her lover's bloody
head in her hand, we think of terrible Chriem-
hilda in the song of the *Nibelungen.* No
words of comfort can penetrate the iron mask
with which she hides her woes.

I stated previously that I should abstain
from all historical and philosophical remarks
concerning Shakespeare's historical plays. The
theme of these plays can never wax old so long
as a fluctuating warfare is kept up betwixt the
necessities of modern industry and the remnants of mediæval feudalism. Here it is less
easy to express a decided opinion than in those
plays treating of Roman history, and possibly
unvarnished truth might not be welcome.
However I will venture on one remark.

I do not sympathise with those German
critics who so heartily agree with the English
when they allude to the French wars, mentioned
by Shakespeare. Here the English had neither
poetical feeling nor right on their side. These
wars were partly the result of a vulgar love of
pillage, shielding itself under worthless excuses

appertaining to the Succession ; and partly they were maintained and carried on for the sake of low mercantile interests. It is the same in our own times, only that in the nineteenth century they fought about coffee and sugar, whereas wool was the subject of discord in the fourteenth and fifteenth centuries.

Michelet correctly remarks in his clever book on French history :

" The explanation of the battles of Crêçy and Poitiers may be found in the offices of London, Bordeaux, and Bruges merchants. The original England and the English race owe their origin to wool and meat. England was a meat factory before it became a great cotton and iron factory. This nation always loved to occupy itself with cattle-breeding and to feed on meat. Thence come their fresh complexions, their strength, their beauty, consisting in short noses and flat occiputs. And here I mention one of my personal impressions ; I had seen London and a great part of England and Scotland ; to me it all seemed more wonderful than comprehensible. I only received a true impression of England's vast extent on my return-journey, when I travelled across from York to Manchester. It was a foggy morning and the country appeared to me not

only surrounded but flooded by the ocean.
Almost half the landscape was bathed in faint
sunshine. The newly-built red-tiled houses
would have stood out almost too vividly against
the rich green lawns, had not the moving sea-
fog somewhat modified these screaming colours.
Flaming factory-chimneys towered over rich
meadows covered with sheep. Cattle-breeding,
agriculture, industry, all were comprised in this
small space, one overtopping the other, one
feeding on the other; the meadows were nour-
ished by the fog, the sheep fattened on the
meadows, human beings lived on blood.

Any one living in this consuming climate
which is always fostering his hunger, must
spend his life in work. Nature compels him
to do this. But he knows how to be avenged;
he makes nature work and subdues her by
means of iron and fire. All England pants
from this warfare. Man appears angry and in
despair. Observe his red face and his restless
and beaming countenance. He might be drunk;
but his head and hand are firm and steady.
He is only intoxicated with blood and strength.
He regards himself as a machine which he
fills with provender until it runs over, for he
has to gain from it as much activity and quick-
ness as possible.

In the middle ages the Englishman was much as he is now : too well fed, driven to work and of warlike propensities lacking industrial occupations.

England, though engaged in agriculture and cattle-breeding, did not as yet possess manufactories. Englishmen supplied the raw material, whilst others made it ready for use. Wool was to be had on one side of the channel, the workman on the other. English cattle-traders and Flemish cloth-manufacturers lived on 'good and inseparable terms, whilst princes fought and quarrelled. A century's war was the result of the French attempt to break this league. The English kings certainly wished to conquer France, but the nation only desired freedom in trade, free import stations and a free market for English wool. The Commons sat in judgment over the king's demands, surrounding a great woolsack, gladly voting him pecuniary and military aid.

There is something very curious in this mixture of industry and chivalry. When Edward, seated at the round table, swore a proud oath that he would conquer France, and when the solemn and absurd knights tied a red bandage across one of their eyes to signify their oath, none of them were foolish enough to make war at their own expense, The simple piety of the Crusaders is a thing of the past. The knights are only mercenaries, paid agents, armed *commis voyageurs* in the pay of London and Ghent merchants.

In order to gain the people's attention Edward has to put himself very much on a level with the people, to divest himself entirely of pride, to flatter the cloth-merchants and weavers, to shake hands with his godfather the brewer Artevelde, and to hold forth from a cattle-trader's writing-desk. Very comic incidents occur in the English tragedies of the fourteenth century. The noblest knights always bore some likeness to Falstaff. In France, Italy, Spain, in the beautiful countries of the South, Englishmen are as greedy as they are brave. We look on at Hercules swallowing an ox. They actually come to feed on the land. But the land avenges itself on them and conquers them with its fruits and its wine. Their princes and armies fare too sumptuously on food and drink, dying of indigestion and dysentery."

Let us compare the French, that moderate people who are less inclined to become drunk with wine than with their inborn enthusiasm, to this mercenary nation of gluttons. This was

ever the cause of their misfortunes, and thus
we see how they succumbed to the English
already in the middle of the fourteenth century
owing to their superabundant chivalry. This
happened at Crêçy where the French are more
to be admired in their defeat than the English
in their victory, which they obtained in un-
chivalrous fashion by means of foot-soldiers.
. . . Up to that time war had been one
great tournament between horsemen of equal
rank ; but at Crêçy the infantry of a new era
makes its appearance, giving an ignoble death-
blow to the cavalry of romance ; the poetry of
warfare vanishes in the prose of a strictly
organised battle-order, and cannons come on to
the scene. The old King of Bohemia, who in
the midst of blindness and old age fought at
this battle as a vassal of France, felt that a new
time was coming, that chivalry was at an end
and that in future horsemen would succumb to
men on foot. He said to his knights ; "I
earnestly beseech you to lead me into the thick
of the fray, so that I may once again beat about
me with a good sword-thrust." They obeyed
him, and binding their horses to his, rushed
with him into the thick of the battle, and next
morning were all found dead on the backs of
their dead horses which were still bound to-

gether. The French fell at Crêçy and Poitiers
like this King of Bohemia with his knights;
they died but they died in their saddles.
England had the victory but France the glory.
Ah yes! Even in defeat the French can throw
their opponents into the shade. Since the days
of Crêçy and Poitiers down to Waterloo, the
triumphs of Englishmen have always been a
disgrace to humanity. In spite of her impartial
coldness Clio remains a woman and has a heart
for chivalry and heroism; and I am assured
that she notes on her memorial tablets with a
heart full of bitter cursing, the victories of the
English nation.

LADY GREY   [*Henry VI. Part III.*]

LADY GREY was a poor widow, who appeared
before Edward in fear and trembling, beseech-
ing him to restore to her children their patri-
mony, which after her husband's death had
come into the possession of their enemies. The
voluptuous king, who cannot shake her modesty,
is so enraptured by her charming tears, that
he places a crown upon her head. History
shows us what troubles for both sprang from
this union.

We wonder whether Shakespeare has kept
true to history in his delineation of this king's

character. I again observe that he could always fill up the gaps of history. His kings are always so true to life, that according to an English author we might frequently imagine that he had all his life been chancellor to any one of the kings he chooses to depict. Another evidence of his trustworthiness may be found in the strong likeness which exists between his kings of ancient date and ours of the present day, and whom, as their contemporaries, we can the more easily criticise.

We may say of this poet what Friedrich Schlegel says of the historian. He is a prophet, casting backward glances on the past. Were it permissible for me to hold up a mirror to one of our most celebrated royal contemporaries, I could show that Shakespeare composed this king's death-warrant not less than two hundred years ago. Indeed, in beholding this great excellent and decidedly grand monarch we are overcome with a certain feeling of horror, such as we feel when we meet any one in the light of day, who has appeared to us in our dreams at night. When eight years ago we saw him riding through the streets of the capital " bowing bareheaded lower than his proud steed's neck," we always thought of those words in which York describes Boling-

broke's entry into London. His cousin, the
Richard II. of a later date, knew him well
always read his character, and once correctly
observed ;

> "Ourself and Bushey, Bagot here and Green,
>   Observed his courtship to the common people ;
>   How he did seem to dive into their hearts
>   With humble and familiar courtesy ;
>   What reverence he did throw away on slaves ;
>   Wooing poor craftsmen with the craft of smiles,
>   And patient underbearing of his fortune,
>   As 'twere to banish their affects with him.
>   Off goes his bonnet to an oyster wench ;
>   A brace of draymen bid God speed him well,
>   And had the tribute of his supple knee,
>   With 'thanks my countrymen, my loving friends.' "

The likeness is indeed terrible. The present
Bolingbroke, who ascended the throne after the
downfall of his royal cousin, gradually retaining
a firm hold over it, appeared just as the Bolingbroke of old ; he is a cunning hero, a cringing
giant, a hypocritical Titan. With terrible and
revolting calmness he keeps his claw enveloped
in a velvet glove ; with this he strokes public
opinion, whilst he eyes his prey from afar and
never pounces down upon it till safely within
reach. May he succeed in conquering his
enemies and preserving peace to the nation
until his death, on which occasion he will

repeat to his son those words long since composed for him by William Shakespeare.

"Come hither, Harry, sit thou by my bed;
  And hear I think the very latest counsel
  That ever I shall breathe.   God knows, my son,
  By what by-paths and indirect crook'd ways
  I met this crown; and I myself know well
  How troublesome it sat upon my head:
  To thee it shall descend with better quiet,
  Better opinion, better confirmation;
  For all the soil of the achievement goes
  With me into the earth: it seemed in me
  But as an honour snatched with boisterous sound;
  And I had many living to upbraid
  My gain of it by their assistances;
  Which daily grew to quarrel and to bloodshed,
  Wounding supposèd peace: all these bold fears
  Thou see'st with peril I have answerèd;
  For all my reign hath been but as a scene
  Acting that argument: and now my death
  Changes the mode; for what in me was purchased
  Falls upon thee in a more fairer sort;
  So thou the garland wear'st successively,
  Yet tho' thou stand'st more sure than I could do,
  Thou art not firm enough, since griefs are green;
  And all my foes which thou must make thy friends
  Have but their stings and teeth newly ta'en out;
  By whose fell working I was first advanced,
  And by whose power I well might lodge a fear
  To be again displayed; which to avoid,
  I cut some off and had a purpose now
  To lead out many to the Holy Land,
  Lest rest and lying still might make them look
  Too near unto my state.   Therefore, my Harry,

Be it thy course to busy giddy minds
With foreign quarrels ; that action hence borne out
May waste the memory of the former days :
More would I but my lungs are wasted so
That strength of speech is utterly denied me,
How came I by the crown, oh ! God forgive ;
And grant it may with thee in true peace live."

LADY ANNE [*Richard III.*]

THE favour of women, as of good fortune, is a free gift ; it comes to us without our knowing how or why. But there are men who by force of an iron will can defy fate, and these obtain their ends by flattery, by striking women with terror, or firing them with pity, or by giving them occasion to sacrifice themselves. This last is a favourite *rôle* with women ; it makes them look well in the eyes of others and gives them tender tearful enjoyment in their solitary hours.

Lady Anne is won by all these qualities. Like honey, flattering words fall from terrible lips . . . That same Richard who inspires her with all the fears of hell, who has murdered her beloved husband and the fatherly friend whom she has just followed to the grave, that Richard flatters her. . . . He orders the pall-bearers to put down the bier in a commanding voice, and in that moment the beautiful sufferer is wooed . . . The lamb beholds the wolf's fangs with horror, but suddenly sweet sounds of flattery issue from the wolf's diaphragm . . . there is a sudden revulsion of feeling in this poor lamb, for the wolf's flattery has an exciting and intoxicating effect. . . . And King Richard speaks of his sorrow and misery, so that Anne cannot refuse him her sympathy, especially as this wild man is not very quarrelsome by nature . . . And the unhappy murderer has a conscience; he speaks of repentance and says that a good self-sacrificing wife may teach him better ways. . . . And Anne decides to become Queen of England.

QUEEN KATHARINE [*Henry VIII.*]

In spite of the great virtues which I have to acknowledge in her, I have an insurmountable dislike to this princess. As a married woman she was a pattern of social fidelity. As a queen she was most dignified and majestic. As a Christian she was virtue personified. But she inspired Dr. Samuel Johnson with a voice to sing her highest praise, and of all the women described by Shakespeare she is his special favourite. He mentions her with tender pathos . . . and this is insufferable. Shakespeare did his best to idealise the good woman but this is in vain, when we perceive that this beer-barrel Dr. Johnson is overcome by tender delight at her sight and runs over in her praise. Were she my wife I could make such praise a ground of separation. Possibly it was not owing to the charms of Anne Bullen, but to some Dr. Johnson of that period, raving about the faithful, dignified, and pious Katharine, that she became estranged from the poor king. Did Thomas More, who with all his excellence was somewhat of a pedant, stiff and indigestible like Dr, Johnson—did he sing her praises too loudly ? His enthusiasm cost the good chancellor somewhat dear, as the king in return secured his entrance into heaven.

I do not know whether most to admire Katharine for putting up with her husband for fifteen entire years, or Henry for putting up with his wife for so long a period ? The king was not only very capricious and passionate and always opposed to his wife's wishes ;—that is often the case in marriages, which nevertheless bear the test of time perfectly until death puts a stop to quarrels—but the king was both a musician and a theologian, and both in finished imperfection. Not long ago I heard a delightfully curious *chorale* composed by him which was about as bad as his treatise *de Septem Sacramentis.* The poor woman must surely have been greatly plagued with his musical compositions and theological writing. His love of plastic art was Henry's best quality, and possibly some of his worst likes and dislikes sprang from his love of the beautiful. Katharine of Arragon was still pretty in her twenty-fourth year, when Henry who was eighteen married her, though she had been his brother's widow. But her beauty probably did not increase with age, especially as her piety drove her to scourge herself, to fast, to keep virgils, and to mortify her flesh in every possible way. Her husband often complained of these ascetic practices, and I also should have found this very objectionable in a wife.

But I have another cause of prejudice; this queen was the daughter of Isabella of Castile and the mother of Bloody Mary. What shall I think of the tree which sprang from such an evil seed and bore such evil fruit?

Even if history bears no trace of her cruelty, the wild haughtiness of her race in which she wishes to be imposing through her rank is displayed on every occasion. In spite of her much-practised Christian humility she is always possessed with well-nigh heathenish rage, if the formalities of customary etiquette are not always strictly observed or if she is denied her royal title. She retained this indelible pride till she breathed her last, and Shakespeare makes her say in her last words :

> " Embalm me,
> Then lay me forth; although unqueened yet like
> A queen and daughter to a king, inter me,
> I can no more."

ANNE BULLEN   [*Henry VIII.*]

It is generally supposed that lovely Anne Bullen's charms first occasioned Henry's qualms of conscience respecting his marriage with Katharine. Even Shakespeare hints at this, and when the new queen appears among the crowd on the coronation day one of the young noblemen exclaims :

> " Heaven bless thee !
> Thou hast the sweetest face I ever looked on—
> Sir, as I have a soul she is an angel ;
> Our king has all the Indies in his arms
> And more and richer when he strains that lady :
> I cannot blame his conscience."

We get an idea of Anne Bullen's beauty when in the following scene the poet describes the enthusiasm which her appearance created at the coronation.

By the minute description which Shakespeare gives of the coronation of Elizabeth's mother, we can see how devotedly he loved his great queen. These details appear to give a sanction to the daughter's right of succession, and it was given to a poet to satisfy the entire public concerning the disputed legitimacy of his queen. And this queen deserved his loving zeal! To her there seemed no sin against royal dignity in permitting the poet to put on the stage all her ancestors, even her own father, with terrible impartiality. And not only as a queen but as a woman she never sets any limits to the rights of poetry. Just as Shakespeare was allowed the greatest freedom of speech in political matters, so also was he permitted to use the boldest words respecting sexual relations. Elizabeth was not offended at the most extravagant and the wittiest manifestations of healthy passion, and this " maiden queen " even desired that Sir John Falstaff should once be put on the stage as a lover. To her witty suggestion we owe the *Merry Wives of Windsor*.

Shakespeare could not bring his English historical plays to a better conclusion than by representing a future of better promise in its swaddling clothes; namely in that scene of

Henry VIII., where the newly-born Elizabeth is carried across the stage.

But has Shakespeare faithfully delineated the character of Henry VIII., his queen's father? Though the truth is less loudly proclaimed than in his other plays he does express it, and the gentler tone he assumes makes all reproaches appear the more impressive. This Henry VIII. was the worst of all kings, for whilst other wicked princes only raged against their enemies, he raged against his friends and his love was always more dangerous than his hate. The marriage stories of this royal Bluebeard are terrible. And we perceive a certain foolish and horrible gallantry in the midst of these horrors. When ordering Anne Bullen's execution, he informed her he had engaged the cleverest executioner in England. The queen thanked him for his tender attention, and placing both her white hands round her neck called out in a gay light-hearted manner; " I have only a thin little neck and I am easy to behead."

The axe with which they beheaded her is not large either. I saw it in the arsenal of the Tower of London, and strange thoughts crept over me as I held it in my hands.

Were I the queen of England that axe should be cast to the bottom of the sea.

LADY MACBETH [*Macbeth*]

FROM the so-called historical plays, I turn to those tragedies which are entirely based on imagination, or which are drawn from old legends and stories. *Macbeth* forms a transition-play to these, and in this play Shakespeare's genius takes its freest and boldest flight. The materials of the play which are not historical are taken from an old legend, and yet the play lays some claim to historic fact as the ancestor of the royal house of England plays a part in it. Macbeth was performed in the reign of James I., who is known to have been a descendant of the Scotch Banquo. Shakespeare took note of this when he introduced into his play several prophecies in honour of the reigning dynasty.

In Macbeth the critics seize the opportunity of dwelling on the difference which is manifested between ancient and modern dramatists in their treatment of the idea of destiny. I only make a passing observation thereupon.

Shakespeare differs from the ancients in his view of destiny just as the sisterhood of witches who appear in his tragedy differ from the soothsaying women who greet Macbeth with the promise of a crown in the old northern legend.

In this these strange women are evidently Valkyrias, terrible goddesses of the upper regions, who hover over battle - fields and prognosticate victory or defeat. They may be considered the real arbiters of human destiny, as this was determined by the result of battles in the warlike north. With Shakespeare they turn into malicious witches ; he divests them of the awful grace of northern witchcraft turning them into hybrid monsters, who act in strange hobgoblin fashion. They are bent on destruction, owing to a spiteful love of mischief or by order of the devil ; they are the servants of evil and whosoever gives ear to their decrees is lost body and soul. The heathen Fates of the ancients, endowed with praiseworthy and magical beneficence have therefore been christianised by Shakespeare. The destruction of his hero is not the result of fore-ordained necessity, something unalterably fixed, like the ancient idea of destiny, but it is traceable to the allurements of hell, which in unseen ways enmesh human hearts. Macbeth is conquered by the power of the devil, the root of all evil.

It is interesting to draw a comparison between Shakespeare's witches and those of other English poets. We see that Shakespeare could not quite lose sight of the ancient heathen conception, and his magical apparitions are therefore infinitely more imposing and respectable than Middleton's witches, who give signs of a more evil and dissolute nature. These practise meaner tricks, only harm the body without being able to touch the soul and at their worst can only call forth in us feelings of jealousy, envy, concupiscence and such-like qualities.

Within the last twelve years in Germany Lady Macbeth's reputation, which for two hundred years was considered extremely bad, has altered considerably to her advantage. Pious Franz Horn remarked in Brockhause's *Conversations-Blatt* that the poor lady had been greatly misunderstood, that she dearly loved her husband, and was endowed with an affectionate spirit. This view was supported by the learned, erudite, and philosophic Ludwig Tieck, and not long after we beheld Madame Stich, billing and cooing sentimentally in the character of Lady Macbeth at the Court Theatre. Many a heart in Berlin was touched by her ·tones and many a beautiful woman wept at the sight of this good Lady Macbeth. This happened, as I said, twelve years ago at the time of the restoration, when love reigned supreme. Since then we are become love's bankrupts, and it is owing to people like the Queen of Scotland, who entirely engrossed our sympathies during the restoration, that we are no longer able to fall desperately in love with many a crowned head, though they may deserve our homage.

I do not know whether Germans still defend the aforenamed lady's character. However much has changed since the July revolution, and possibly, even in Berlin, people have come to see that the good Lady Macbeth may be a very beast.

OPHELIA [*Hamlet*]

HERE we have poor Ophelia loved by Hamlet of Denmark. She was a beautiful fair girl and even when I wished to go to Wittenberg to pay my adieux to her father I was touched by the tender magic of her voice. The old gentleman was good enough to send me on my way with all the good maxims not put in practice by himself, and at last he summoned Ophelia to bring wine as a parting beverage. On the approach of the dear child holding the salver gracefully and modestly, and gazing on me fixedly with her large glistening eyes, I became

confused and seized an empty glass instead of
a full one. She smiled at my mistake. Then
already her smile was wonderfully bright and
a melting tenderness flitted across her lips,
which proceeded possibly from kissing elves
who kept watch at the corners of her mouth.

After my return from Wittenberg when I
was again welcomed by Ophelia's smile my
scholastic subtleties forsook me and I only
pondered on the delightful thought,—" what
is the meaning of that smile, that voice, of those
tender, mysterious tones as of a flute? Whence
do those eyes receive their beneficent beams?
Are they reflections of heaven, or does heaven
only reflect those eyes? Is that smile connected with the silent music of the spheres, or
is it only an earthly sign of heavenly harmonies?" One delightful day which we spent in
the palace gardens of Elsinore, joking and
tenderly prattling, our hearts in the first bloom
of love. . . . I can never forget how
wretchedly poor the song of the nightingales
seemed in comparison with Ophelia's heavenly
voice, and how miserably shy the flowers looked
with their bright and solemn faces when compared with Ophelia's lovely smile. Like a
lovely spirit her slender form hovered beside
me.

Ah yes ! it is the curse of weak mortals that they always begin by letting out their spleen on their best and dearest friends when they have had to suffer some terrible injustice. Poor Hamlet began by disturbing his own reason, that precious jewel, and owing to a feigned confusion of ideas rushed into the awful abyss of actual madness paining his poor Ophelia with bitter sarcasms. . . . Poor thing, to crown it all he stabbed her father, taking him for a rat. . . . And then her reason also forsook her ! . . . But her madness is not so terrible, so ominously brooding as that of Hamlet, it rather seems to rock her sick brain to sleep with tender melodies . . . her soft voice melts into song and her thoughts are entwined with abundant, flowers. She sings and plaits wreaths as she crowns herself and smiles blissfully, poor child ! . . .

"There is a willow-grass aslant a brook,
 That shows his hoar leaves in the glassy stream ;
 There with fantastic garlands did she come
 Of crow flowers, nettles, daisies and long purples
 That liberal shepherds give a grosser name
 But our cold maids do dead men's fingers call them :
 There on the pendant boughs her coronet weeds
 Clambering to hang, an envious sliver broke ;
 When down her weedy trophies and herself
 Fell in the weeping brook. Her clothes spread wide

And, mermaid like, awhile they bore her up;
Which time she chanted snatches of old tunes,
As one incapable of her own distress,
Or like a creature native and indued
Unto that element : but long it could not be
Till that her garments, heavy with their drink,
Pulled the poor wretch from her melodious lay
To muddy death."

But why relate this sad story! From your earliest childhood you have all known it, and many a time you have wept for Hamlet of Denmark who loved poor Ophelia. He loved her more than a thousand brothers with all their love put together could have done, and he was driven mad because his father's ghost appeared to him, and because the world was out of joint and he too weak to set it right. He lost his reason because he had forgotten the meaning of action through much thinking in German Wittenberg, because he had to choose between going mad or doing a desperate deed, and because altogether he had as a man distinctly mad tendencies.

We know Hamlet as well as our own faces which often appear to us in the glass, and which nevertheless we know less thoroughly than we might imagine ; for were we to meet anyone precisely like ourselves in the streets we should stare instinctively with secret dismay at the strange well-known features, without being aware that we had looked upon ourselves.

CORDELIA [*King Lear*]

In this play, says an English writer, there are traps and snares for the reader. Another remarks that this play is a labyrinth in which the critic may go astray if he is not strangled by the Minotaur who there resides, were he only to use his critical pruning-knife in self-defence. And indeed it is an awkward thing to criticise Shakespeare whose words constantly strike us as the sharpest criticism of our own words and acts. Therefore we can hardly pass judgment on this play where his genius mounts to a bewildering height.

I only venture to approach the portals of Shakespeare's wonderful edifice—the *mise-en-scène* which immediately strikes us. We leave both our workaday and holiday thoughts behind us in the very first scenes and find ourselves surrounded by the great events which are to overwhelm and purify our minds. Thus Macbeth commences with the meeting of the witches, and not only is the Scotch captain who appears before us in the flush of victory enslaved by their prophecy but our own hearts are unswervingly taken captive as we watch the play until all is fulfilled and ended. At the commencement of *Macbeth* the wild and confusing horror of the bloody world of enchantment takes possession of us, and equally so in the opening scenes of Hamlet do we shudder with horror at the pale spirit-world, and until all is over and the air of Denmark is again purged of the human corruption which pervades it, we cannot rid ourselves of ghostly night-thoughts and of the nightmare of mysterious fear.

In the first scenes of *King Lear* we watch with interest how the life-history of others begins proceeds and ends. The poet here presents us with a play more horrible than all the horrors of the world of enchantment or of spirits. He shows us human passion breaking through all reasonable bounds, raging in the terrible majesty of royal madness, and emulating outraged nature at her wildest. But I think the wonderful power and playful fancy with which Shakespeare could always manage his materials ends here. In this play he is far more governed by his genius than in *Macbeth* and *Hamlet*, where with artistic calm he could bring in juxtaposition the brightest sparks of wit and the darkest shadow of spiritual night, painting the happiest still-life in close proximity to the wildest acts. Yes, in *Macbeth* we are smiled upon by quiet and contented nature; swallows build their quiet nests in the eaves of that very castle where the bloodiest deed was accomplished; throughout the play a pleasant Scotch summer not too hot or cold enwraps us, everywhere we behold beautiful trees and green foliage and at last a whole forest marches up to us; Birnam Wood comes to Dunsinane. In *Hamlet* also the loveliness of nature presents a contrast to the solemnity of events. Though the hero's heart remains dark as night, the sun in spite of it rises again with a tender flush. Polonius is an amusing fool; they play at comedies with one another and poor Ophelia sits beneath green trees and makes wreaths of bright blooming flowers. But these contrasts betwixt nature and the action of the play are not to be found in *King Lear* and the unbridled elements vie with the mad king in their howling and their fury. Can an unusual moral event have any influence over so-called dead matter? Is there an outward visible and intentional harmony betwixt this and the human mind? Did Shakespeare recognise this and intend to represent it?

As we said before, already in the first scene of this tragedy we find ourselves plunged into the thick of events and a sharp eye can prognosticate the storm however clear the sky. King Lear's mind is overshadowed by a small cloud which in time will thicken to the blackest spiritual night. He who parts with everything in this manner is already mad. In the opening scene we get to know the characters of the daughters as well as the mind of the hero, and Cordelia's silent tenderness greatly touches us at the outset. She is a modern Antigone surpassing her ancient sister in warmth of feeling, —a pure spirit as the king only begins to perceive in his madness. Is she perfectly pure ? I can see in her some of her father's obstinacy. But true love is very timid and hates mere verbiage ; it can only weep and bleed to death. There is great tenderness in Cordelia's sorrowfully bitter allusion to the hypocrisy of her sisters, and it resembles the irony occasionally made use of by the Gospel-Hero, the master of charity. She unburdens herself of her righteous anger and proves her noble mind by the words :

"Sure I shall never marry like my sisters.
To love my father all."

JULIET   [*Romeo and Juliet*]

EVERY play of Shakespeare has indeed its special soil, period, and local peculiarity. Just as the characters in these plays, so also have the heaven and earth therein depicted their special physiognomy. In *Romeo and Juliet* we have suddenly crossed the Alps and find ourselves in the beautiful garden of Italy.

" Know'st thou the land where the pale lemon blows ?
  And midst dark glistening leaves the golden orange glows? "

Shakespeare chose sunny Verona as the scene of those bold deeds of love which he meant to depict in *Romeo and Juliet*. Not the above-named pair, but love itself is the hero of this play. With the temerity of youth love comes on to the stage, fronting every inimical condition and overcoming everything . . . for during the great battle it does not fear taking refuge in death—that most terrible but also most certain of boon-fellows. Love in league with death cannot be overcome—it is the highest and most victorious of passions ! But its all-subduing might consists in its bound-less generosity, in its transcendent unselfish-ness, in its contempt of the life which it burns to sacrifice. There is no yesterday in its eyes, and it thinks of no to-morrow. . . . Only the present moment is its desire, but this must be sacrificed wholly without stint or grudge

. . . None of it shall be hoarded up for the future, and it despises the warmed up remnants of the past. . . . *Night in front of me, night at back of me.* . . . It is a pillar of fire walking between two dark hosts. . . . Whence comes it ? . . . From unimaginable tiny sparks. . . . How does it end ? . . . It leaves no trace and we fail to understand where it is gone . . . the wilder it burns the sooner does it become extinct . . . but that does not hinder it from sacrificing all to its burning desires as though its heat were of everlasting duration.

Woe betide us if this great fire breaks out a second time. We need the belief in its immortality, and we know by saddest experience that eventually it feeds upon itself . . . thence the difference in the kind of melancholy, produced by a first and a second love . . . In the first case we think our passion can only cease with tragic death, and really if the threatening difficulties cannot otherwise be overcome we easily resolve to step into the tomb with our beloved. . . . But in the case of our second love we remember that our wildest and happiest feelings change gradually into a tame luke-warmness and that the day will come when we shall gaze indifferently on those lips, eyes, and

limbs, which now fill us with a strange delight
. . . Ah! this thought is sadder than any
presentiment of death . . . It is a hopeless
feeling when in the midst of passionate excite-
ment we think of future emptiness and luke-
warmness, and know by experience that these
highly poetical heroic passions will come to a
miserable end! . . .

These highly poetical heroic passions!
They behave like stage-beauties, *rouge* their
cheeks, dress gorgeously, and wander about
proudly, declaiming in measured iambics . . .
but when the curtain falls the poor beauty
returns to her workaday clothes, washes the
rouge from her cheeks, hands over her jewels
to the master of the wardrobe and drags
herself along, hanging on the arm of the first-
come quarter-sessions clerk whilst she talks
bad German, creeps with him into an attic,
yawns and lies down snoring, no longer listen-
ing to the words,—" you acted divinely, on
my honour!" . . .

I cannot venture to impute any blame to
Shakespeare. I admire him for allowing
Romeo to be in love with Rosalind at the
commencement before he is introduced to
Juliet. Although this second love seizes him
heart and soul, his mind is haunted by a certain

doubt which reveals itself in ironic words, re-
minding us of Hamlet. Or does a man love
more strongly the second time just because he
then loves with a better knowledge of himself ?
To a woman a second love is impossible for
her nature is too delicate to survive a second
time this terrible upheaval of her mind. Look
at Juliet. Could she endure a second time
superhuman delights and horrors, so as to drink
her misery to the dregs in spite of all her fears ?
I think this poor fond creature, this poor victim
of the great passion had had enough with once.
Juliet loves for the first time and loves with
the strength which belongs to a healthy body
and soul. She is fourteen years old, which in
Italy is as much as seventeen years of northern
reckoning. She is a rosebud opening in young
splendour before our eyes, preparing for Romeo's embrace. She has not learned what
love is from secular or religious books ; the sun
has told it her, and the moon has repeated it
and her own heart echoed the refrain when she
believed herself alone at night. But Romeo
stood beneath the balcony and heard her speak,
taking her at her word. Her love is charac-
terised by truth and health. The maiden
breathes forth health and truth, and very touching are the words in which she says :

"Thou know'st the mask of night is on my face,
Else would a maiden blush bepaint my cheek
For that which thou hast heard me speak to-night.
Fain would I dwell on form, fain, fain deny
What I have spoke, but farewell compliment !
Dost thou love me? I know thou wilt say 'aye';
And I will take thy word : yet if thou swear'st,
Thou may'st prove false ; at lover's perjuries,
They say Jove laughs. Oh, gentle Romeo,
If thou dost love, pronounce it faithfully ;
Or if thou think'st I am too quickly won,
I'll frown and be perverse and say thee nay,
So thou wilt woo ; but else not for the world ;
In truth, fair Montague, I am too fond ;
And therefore thou may'st think my 'haviour' light :
But trust me, gentleman, I'll prove more true
Than those that have more cunning to be strange,
I should have been more strange, I must confess,
But that thou overheard'st, ere I was 'ware,
My true love's passion : therefore pardon me ;
And not impute this yielding to light love,
Which the dark night hath so discoverèd."

DESImimiDESDEMONA [Othello]

I OBSERVED in passing that Romeo's character
had in it some of Hamlet's characteristics. And
in truth here and there a tinge of northern
solemnity overshadows this ardent soul. In
comparing Desdemona to Juliet we also perceive this northern element ; she remains herself in the midst of her wildest passion and
controls herself with clear self-consciousness.

Juliet loves, thinks and acts. Desdemona loves, feels and obeys, not her own will but her stronger instinct. Her excellence consists in this : that wickedness can never master her noble nature as virtue can. She would surely have remained in her father's palace a timid child devoted to household duties, had not the Moor's voice sounded in her ears, and though she dropped her eyelids she felt his glance in his words and in his stories or, as she expressed it, "in his mind"; and this suffering, noble, beautiful, pale spirit-face, bewitched her irresistibly. Her father, the wise senator Brabantio, was right; some mighty magic drew this shy and tender child towards the Moor, making her fearless at the sight of the ugly black mask which the common crowd took for Othello's real face. . . .

Juliet's love is active, Desdemona's passive. She is the sun-flower not knowing that she always turns toward the sun, a true daughter of the south, tender, sensitive, patient, like those slender great-eyed women who smile upon us from Sanskrit poems with their lovely and tender faces. I am always reminded of Kalidasa, the Indian Shakespeare, and his *Sacontala* when I think of her.

Possibly the English engraver has thrown

too strong an expression of passion into Desdemona's face.   But I fancy I have already remarked that there is a pleasurable interest in drawing comparisons between faces and characters.   At any rate this face is very beautiful and especially charming to the writer of these pages, as it reminds him of that great beauty, who hitherto is only known to his inner consciousness and who, heaven be praised, never regarded him too critically!

" Her father loved me, oft invited me ;
   Still questioned me the story of my life,
   From year to year, the battles, sieges, fortunes,
   That I have passed.
   I ran it through, even from my boyish days
   To the very moment that he bade me tell it :
   Wherein I spake of most disastrous chances,
   Of moving accidents by flood and field ;
   Of hair-breadth 'scapes ; i' th' imminent deadly breach
   Of being taken by the insolent foe,
   And sold to slavery ; of my redemption thence
   And 'portance in my travels' history :
   Wherein of antres vast and deserts idle,
   Rough quarries, rocks and hills whose heads touch heaven,
   It was my hint to speak—such was the process :
   And of the cannibals that each other eat,
   The Anthropophagi and men whose heads
   Do grow beneath their shoulders.   This to hear
   Would Desdemona seriously incline :
   But still the house-affairs would draw her thence,
   Which ever as she could with haste despatch,

She'd come again and with a greedy ear
Devour up my discourse :—which I observing,
Took once a pliant hour ; and found good means
To draw from her a prayer of earnest heart,
That I would all my pilgrimage dilate
Whereof by parcels she had something heard,
But not intentively : I did consent ;
And often did beguile her of her tears,
When I did speak of some distressful stroke
That my youth suffered.   My story being done,—
She gave me for my pains a world of sighs :
She swore—in faith 'twas strange, 'twas passing strange,
'Twas pitiful, 'twas wondrous pitiful :
She wished she had not heard it ; yet she wished
That heaven had made her such a man : she thanked me ;
And bade me if I had a friend that loved her,
I should but teach him how to tell my story,
And that would woo her.   Upon this hint I spake ;
She loved me for the dangers I had passed ;
And I loved her that she did pity them."

This tragedy is considered one of Shakespeare's latest works, as *Titus Andronicus* is
considered the earliest.   There as here the
poet loves to dwell on the passion with which
an ugly Moor could inspire a beautiful woman.
The mature man returned to a problem which
had engaged his youthful attention.   Did he
explain the riddle ?   And is the solution as
true as it is beautiful ?   A weary sadness
sometimes creeps over me when I think that
possibly honest Iago with his wicked jokes

concerning Desdemona's love for the Moor may have some right on his side. But Othello's words in which he refers to his wife's moist hands are to me more distasteful than anything else.

There is in the *Arabian Nights* just as strange and striking an example of love for a Moor as we get in *Titus Andronicus* and in *Othello*. In this case a beautiful princess who is also a wizard, after putting her husband into a statue-like trance gives him a daily flogging, because he has murdered her lover, an ugly negro. The princess, crying out in her agony at the negro's death-bed, excites our pity. She appears to keep him alive by her magic art whilst she covers him with despairing kisses; and she would like by a magic greater yet, by love itself to awaken him out of this semi-trance to a yet fuller life. This story of a passionate and mysterious love related in the *Arabian Nights* struck my fancy while still a boy.

JESSICA   [*Merchant of Venice*]

WHEN I saw this play acted at Drury Lane a beautiful pale Englishwoman standing beside me burst into tears at the end of the fourth act, crying out several times, "the poor man is wronged." She had a refined classical face and large dark eyes which I could not forget for they had wept for Shylock.

On account of these tears I must place *The Merchant of Venice* among Shakespeare's tragedies although he intended it as a comedy surrounding it by merry masks satyrs and cupids. Possibly Shakespeare thought it would please the public were he to represent a greedy were-wolf, a dread mythical creature thirsting for blood, thereby losing his daughter and his ducats, besides exciting general ridicule. But the poet's genius, the world-spirit which reigns in him, always supersedes his individual will. Thus it came to pass that notwithstanding the obvious caricature which Shylock presents, Shakespeare has justified in him an unfortunate race whom Providence for some secret cause has burdened with the hatred of the low and high-born populace, and who has not always consented to return love for hate.

But what do I say ? Shakespeare's genius rises above the mean quarrels of two parties entertaining opposite beliefs, and his play does not actually represent either Jews or Christians but oppressors and oppressed. We also hear the madly painful shouts of joy whenever the latter are able to pay back with interest the

injuries inflicted on them by their proud tor-
turers.   There is not the slightest trace of
religious differences in this play, and in Shylock, Shakespeare represents a character whose
nature it is to hate his enemy.   In a similar
manner we find that Antonio and his friends
are by no means apostles of that divine gospel
which commands men to love their enemies.
Shylock replies to the man wishing to borrow
money of him ;

" Signor Antonio, many a time and oft
   In the Rialto you have rated me
   About my moneys and my usances :
   Still have I borne it with a patient shrug ;
   For sufferance is the badge of all our tribe :
   You call me misbeliever, cut-throat dog ;
   And spit upon my Jewish gabardine,
   And all for use of that which is mine own.
   Well then it now appears you need my help :
   Go to then ; you come to me and you say,
   ' Shylock, we would have moneys ' :—you say so ;
   You that did void your rheum upon my beard,
   And foot me as you spurn a stranger cur
   Over your threshold : moneys is your suit.
   What should I say to you ?   Should I not say
   ' Hath a dog money ? is it possible
   A cur can lend three thousand ducats ? '   Or
   Shall I bend low, and in a bondman's key,
   With bated breath, and whispering humbleness,
   Say this,—
   ' Fair Sir, you spit on me on Wednesday last ;

You spurned me such a day ; another time,
You called me dog ; and for these courtesies
I'll lend you thus much moneys ' ? "

And Antonio answers :

"I am as like to call thee so again,
To spit on thee again, to spurn thee too."

Have we here an example of christian love !
Christianity would have been satirised had
Shakespeare typified it by Shylock's enemies,
men who hardly deserved to loosen his shoe-
latchets. The bankrupt Antonio is a weak-
spirited mortal without energy, without power
to hate, and therefore without power to love, a
dull worm whose flesh was really not good for
much else than to serve as "bait for fish."
Besides this he certainly does not return the
fleeced Jew his three thousand ducats. Neither
does Bassanio, who according to an English
critic is a regular fortune-hunter, return him his
money ; this man borrows money for the purpose of setting himself up in grand style to
marry a wealthy wife and to obtain a rich
dowry, for he says to his friend :

" 'Tis not unknown to you, Antonio,
How much I have disabled mine estate,
By something showing a more swelling port
Than my faint means would grant continuance :

Nor do I now make moan to be abridged
From such a noble rate ; but my chief care,
Is to come fairly off from the great debts,
Wherein my time, something too prodigal,
Hath left me gaged. . . . "

As to Lorenzo, he is an accomplice in a most infamous robbery by which according to Prussian law he would be condemned to fifteen years' penal servitude after being branded and put in the pillory, although he had a liking for the beauties of nature for moonlight scenes and music as well as for jewels and ducats. The other noble Venetians, Antonio's friends, also seem to regard money with favour and they have naught but words, coined air for their poor friend in the midst of his misfortunes. Our good pietist Franz Horn remarks with perfect truth, though somewhat feebly, " we may well ask the question here, how was it possible for Antonio to be so overwhelmed by his misfortunes ? All Venice knew and valued him, his good friends were informed of the terrible bond and knew besides that the Jew would not retract a word. Yet they let day after day slip by until the three months are gone, and with them every hope of deliverance. It would surely have been comparatively easy for those good friends who appeared to surround the regal merchant in crowds, to collect three thousand ducats in order to save a human life, and such a life! But these things are always rather inconvenient and so the dear good friends do nothing—nothing whatever—because they are only so-called friends, or, if you will, semi or three-quarter friends. They greatly pity the excellent merchant who formerly entertained them so well, but they do this in a calm manner and revile Shylock to their heart's content heaping bitter words on him. This also they can do without incurring any risks, and they then probably all imagine that they have done their duty. Much as we are bound to hate Shylock we can understand even him for somewhat despising these people, which he has every right to do. Indeed, eventually he seems to mistake the absent Gratiano for these others when he alludes in cutting words to the previous inaction and present bluster classing him with them thus,

"Till thou canst rail the seal from off my bond
Thou but offend'st thy lungs to speak so loud;
Repair thy wit, good youth, or it will fall
To cureless ruin—I stand here for law!"

Or are we to take Lancelot Gobbo as a type of christianity? Oddly enough Shakespeare has nowhere expressed himself more decidedly on this subject than in a conversation between this rogue and his mistress. In reply to Jessica's words

"I shall be saved by my husband; he hath made me a christian"

Lancelot Gobbo answers :

"Truly the more to blame he; we were christians enow before; e'en as many as could well live, one by ancther. This making of christians will raise the price of hogs; if we grow all to be pork-eaters, we shall not shortly have a rasher on the coals for money."

Indeed with the exception of Portia, the character of Shylock is the most worthy in the play. He loves money and makes no secret of his passion crying it out on the open market place. . . . But something he prizes more than money, namely the easing of his wounded spirit, the just vengeance for inexpressible injuries, and though they offer him ten times the amount of the borrowed sum he refuses it. He will not accept the three thousand even ten times three thousand ducats, if instead he can procure a pound of his enemy's flesh. Salarino asks him ;

"What wilt thou with this flesh?"

and he answers :

"To bait fish withal: if it will feed nothing else, it will feed my revenge. He hath disgraced me and hindered me half a million; laughed at my losses, mocked at my gains, scorned my nation, thwarted my bargains, cooled my friends, heated mine enemies; and what's his reason? I am a Jew. Hath not a Jew eyes? Hath not a Jew hands, organs, dimensions, senses, affections, passions? fed with the same food, hurt with the same weapons, subject to the same diseases, healed by the same means, warmed and cooled by the same winter and summer as a Christian is? If you prick us, do we not bleed? If you tickle us, do we not laugh? if you poison us, do we not die? and if you wrong us, shall we not revenge? if we are like you in the rest, we will resemble you in that. If a Jew wrong a Christian, what is his humility? revenge: if a Christian wrong a Jew, what should his sufferance be by Christian example? why revenge. The villainy you teach me I will execute; and it shall go hard but I will better the instruction."

Yes indeed though Shylock loves his money there are things he prizes infinitely more, among other things his daughter; "Jessica, my child." Though he curses her in overwhelming and passionate anger, longing to see her dead at his feet with the jewels in her ears and the ducats in her coffin, he loves her nevertheless more than all his jewels and his ducats. Thrust out of public life and christian society into the narrow limits of household joys, the poor Jew found himself entirely dependant on

family ties, and these assume in him patheti-
cally tender proportions. He would not have
given away the turquoise ring once given him
by his wife Lea for a "forest of monkeys."
When in the court of justice Bassanio addresses the following words to Antonio :

> " Antonio, I am married to a wife
> Which is as dear to me as life itself ;
> But life itself, my wife, and all the world,
> Are not with me esteemed above thy life :
> I would lose all, ay sacrifice them all
> Here to this devil, to deliver you."

And when Gratiano adds :

> " I have a wife whom I protest I love :
> I would she were in heaven, so she could
> Entreat some power to change this currish Jew."

Then Shylock begins to tremble for the fate
of his daughter who has married among people
who can sacrifice their wives to their friends,
and he says to himself in an aside and not
aloud :

> " These be the Christian husbands ! I have a daughter
> Would any of the stock of Barabbas
> Had been her husband rather than a Christian ! "

This passage, these silent words, are beautiful
Jessica's death warrant. It was no loveless
father whom she deserted, robbed and betrayed

. . . Oh disgraceful betrayal! She even makes common cause with Shylock's enemies, and when at Belmont they slander him, Jessica does not look down, the colour does not leave her cheeks and she utters base words concerning her father . . . Oh abominable outrage! She has no soul, only the mind of an adventuress. She found the strict honourable home of the embittered Jew tedious, until it seemed to her a hell. The merry sound of drums and fifes had too great attractions for her frivolous mind! Did Shakespeare mean to depict a Jewess? No indeed, he only describes a daughter of Eve, one of those beautiful birds who finding themselves fledged, flutter away from the parental nest to the beloved mate. Desdemona followed the Moor, Imogene followed Posthumus in like manner! It is the custom of women. We perceive in Jessica a certain timid shame which she cannot overcome when she has to dress in boy's clothes. Perhaps in this we may recognise the mysterious shyness peculiar to her race owing to which quality its daughters possess a special charm! Possibly the chastity of the Jews has its root in the dislike they always manifested towards that oriental worship of the senses and sensuality. This used to thrive abundantly among their neighbours the Egyptians, Phœnicians, Assyrians and Babylonians, and to the present day maintains its position undergoing various transformations. The Jews are a pure and temperate race, I might almost call them a people devoted to abstract thought, and in purity of morals they closely approach the Germanic races. Possibly the purity of Jewish and Germanic women is not of much account, but it impresses us as something very lovely, graceful and touching. We weep at the sight of those women who after the defeat of their Cimbrian and Teuton husbands implore Marius to hand them over as slaves to the priestesses of Vesta rather than to his soldiers.

We are struck by the close relationship which exists between these two moral peoples, the Jews and the Germans. It did not come about in historic fashion because the bible, that great family chronicle of the Jews, served as a textbook for the whole Germanic race, nor yet because the Jews and the Germans were always the unrelenting enemies of the Romans and therefore naturally in league with one another. There is a deeper reason, and both nations were originally so alike that ancient Palestine might be regarded as an eastern Germany just as the Germany of to-day might be regarded as

the native soil of God's word, the home of
prophecy and the stronghold of pure spiritu-
ality.

But not only does Germany resemble Palestine, the rest of Europe is placing itself on a
level with the Jews. I say " on a level with,"
for the Jews always bore within themselves that
modern principle which is only now becoming
visibly prominent in the nations of Europe.

The Greeks and Romans were passionately
attached to the soil, to their fatherland. The
northern intruders of a later date who settled
down among Greeks and Romans, attached
themselves to the persons of their respective
chieftains, and in place of the patriotism of
ancient times we get in the middle ages faithful
vassals paying allegiance to their sovereign.
But from of old the Jews obeyed only the law,
abstract thought, like our republicans of the
present day, who regard neither country nor
king, but who worship the law. Ah yes!
Cosmopolitanism had its origin on the shores
of Judæa, and though, as we heard before, that
Hamburg dealer in spices was filled with con-
cern, Christ was nevertheless a true Jew, and
founded the gospel of humanity. In allusion
to Jewish republicanism I remember to have
read in Josephus of certain republicans at

Jerusalem who resisted, and bravely fought against the royalist Herodians, refusing every man the title of "Sir" and hating Roman absolutism with a deep hatred. Their creed was liberty and equality. Ah! the delusion of it!

But what is the final reason of that hatred which exists at the present day in Europe between those disciples of the mosaic law and the gospel of Christ and of which the poet gives us such a terrible picture in the *Merchant of Venice* when he puts abstract things into concrete form? Is it the old enmity between brother and brother begun by Cain and Abel at the world's commencement concerning the different ways of praising God? Or is religion only the excuse and do men hate one another for the sake of hating one another, as they love one another for the sake of loving one another? Who, in this enmity is at fault? As an answer to this question I will quote some words from a private letter which is a vindication of Shylock's enemies as well as of him.

"I do not blame the hatred with which the multitude persecute the Jews; I only condemn the grievous errors which gave rise to this hatred. The common people are always right as regards the cause, there is always a correct instinct at the bottom of their dislikes as of their likes ; but they do not know how to formulate their ideas correctly and their anger generally affects the scapegoat of wrong conditions of time and place, the person rather than the cause. The people are poor, they cannot procure the means of a pleasurable existence, and though the ministers of a state-religion assure them "that we are on earth to deny ourselves and to obey the powers that be, in spite of hunger and thirst"—they not-withstanding have a secret longing to procure themselves enjoyment, and they hate those who having the means to procure these things hoard them in their boxes and safes. They hate the rich and rejoice when they can devote themselves heart and soul to this hatred in the name of religion. The common people always hated in the Jews the owners of the money-bags ; always golden coin caused the lightnings of popular anger to descend on the Jews. And age by age it belonged to the spirit of the times to make this hatred its watchword. In the middle ages this watchword assumed the gloomy form of the catholic church, and they killed the Jews and plundered their homes "because Christ had been crucified." This was as logical as the behaviour of those black Christians of San Domingo, who at the time of the massacres ran about with a crucifix calling out in their fanaticism ;

" Les blancs l'ont tué, tuons nous les blancs."

You laugh at those poor negroes, my friends ; but I assure you at that time the West Indian planters did not laugh. They were put to the sword in revenge for the death of Christ, much as some centuries previously the European Jews had been massacred. But the black Christians of San Domingo also had right on their side ! The white men spent their time idly in the lap of luxury, whilst the negroes had to work for them in the sweat of their black brows, receiving as a reward a small supply of rice and many floggings ; the negroes represented the common people !

We no longer live in the middle ages and the common people are growing more enlightened. They do not kill the Jews on the spur of the moment or cast a religious halo over their hatred. We can no longer lay claim to this childlike, devoted faith ; the traditional hatred clothes itself in modern phraseology and the mob in club-houses as in parliaments holds forth against the Jews with its mercantile, industrial, scientific or even philosophical arguments. Only consummate hypocrites give their hatred the colour of religion and persecute the Jews for Christ's sake ; the majority openly confess that material interests are at the bottom of it all, and they place every possible barrier in the way of those Jews who wish to turn their industrial capacities to account. Here in Frankfort only twenty-four professing Jews may marry so that they may not multiply too fast, lest there should arise too strong a competition betwixt them and Christian merchants. This explains why the Jews are hated ; we can perceive in this enmity no trace of the sad and fanatical monk-like mien, but we recognise the limp and enlightened features of the shop-keeper, afraid of being out-done in his trade by the mercantile mind of the Israelite.

Are the Jews to blame however that this mercantile spirit has assumed in them such alarming proportions ? It has its origin in that absurd idea of the middle ages when trade was considered a thing of slight importance, and when business, even money transactions, were looked upon as something ignoble and disgraceful. Therefore those portions of trade which had to do with gain, especially monetary transactions were placed in the hands of the Jews, thus they necessarily became the cleverest bankers and merchants, being excluded from all other crafts. They were forced into growing rich and their wealth made them hated; and though Christians have given up their prejudices concerning trade and have become as great rogues and as wealthy as the Jews, the latter are still pursued by the hatred of the multitude, which has been handed down from generation to generation. The people continue to consider themselves representatives of the moneyed classes and hate them in proportion. You perceive in the world's history both are right; both "hammer and anvil."

PORTIA   [*Merchant of Venice*]

"Critics have been apparently so dazzled and engrossed by the amazing character of Shylock that Portia has received less than justice at their hands; while the fact is that Shylock is not a finer or more finished character in his way than Portia is in hers. These two splendid figures are worthy of each other —worthy of being placed together within the same rich frame-work of enchanting poetry and glorious and graceful forms. She hangs beside the terrible, inexorable Jew, the brilliant lights

of her character set off by the shadowy power
of his, like a magnificent beauty-breathing
Titian by the side of a gorgeous Rembrandt.

Portia is endued with her own share of those
delightful qualities which Shakespeare has
lavished on many of his female characters ;
but besides the dignity, the sweetness and
tenderness which should distinguish her sex
generally, she is individualized by qualities
peculiar to herself ; by her high mental powers,
her enthusiastic temperament, her decision of
purpose and her buoyancy of spirit. These
are innate ; she has other distinguishing qualities more external and which are the result
of the circumstances in which she is placed.
Thus she is the heiress of a princely name and
countless wealth ; a train of obedient pleasures
have ever waited round her ; and from infancy
she has breathed an atmosphere redolent of
perfume and blandishment. Accordingly there
is a commanding grace a high-bred airy ele-
gance, a spirit of magnificence in all that she
does and says as one to whom splendour has
been familiar from her very birth. She treads
as though her footsteps had been among
marble palaces, beneath roofs of fretted gold,
o'er cedar floors and pavements of jasper and
porphyry, amid gardens full of statues and

flowers and fountains and haunting music.
She is full of penetrative wisdom, and genuine
tenderness and lively wit ; but as she has never
known want, or grief, or fear, or disappoint-
ment, her wisdom is without a touch of the
sombre or the sad ; her affections are all mixed
up with faith and hope and joy, and her wit
has not a particle of malevolence or causticity!"

The above words are taken from Mrs.
Jameson's work entitled *Moral, Poetical and
Historical Women*. In this book only Shakespeare's characters are discussed and the quo-
tation gives us an insight into the mind of
this authoress, probably a Scotchwoman. Her
words concerning Portia as contrasted with
Shylock are as beautiful as they are true. If
we consider Shylock in the usual way, as a
type of that stern, serious, inartistic Judæa,
Portia appears on the other hand as a type of
those after-blossoms of Greek intellect which
in the sixteenth century spread their beautiful
scent from Italy over the world, and which we
now love and revere under the name of the
Renaissance. Portia also represents bright
happiness as contrasted with gloomy misfortune, which we see typified in Shylock. All
her thoughts are blooming, rosy, and pure ; her
speech is penetrated with warm happiness and

her similes, which she generally borrows from mythology, are full of beauty. In Shylock's thoughts and words, borrowed only from old testament metaphors, we get a dismal, pungent and ugly contrast. His wit is spasmodic and pungent, he borrows his metaphors from loathsome objects and his very words are compressed discords, shrill and hissing. Men resemble their homes. We perceive how this servant of Jehovah will not suffer either an image of God, or of man made in God's image, to enter his "honourable house"; he even shuts out every sound from the hearing thereof, namely from the windows, so that sounds of heathen mummery shall not gain entrance there . . . in the beautiful palace at Belmont, on the other hand, we find a luxurious and ideal country home surrounded by light and music. Adorned suitors wander about joyfully among pictures, marble statues and high laurels, dreaming of love's mysteries, whilst Signora Portia reigns over them in all her glory, resplendent as a goddess, "golden hair adorning her temples."

By force of contrast the two chief figures in the play become so individualised that we positively believe them to be actual human beings, instead of a poet's fantastic creations.

To us they appear still more life-like than ordinary mortals, as neither time nor death can alter them and their hearts are quickened by immortal pulsations, by divine poetry. When we visit Venice and wander through the Doge's Palace we know very well that we shall not meet Marino Falieri either in the senators' hall or on the grand staircase ;—the arsenal may remind us of old Dandolo, but we shall not seek out the blind hero in any of the golden galleys ;—possibly for a moment we may think of proud Carmagnole when at the corner of Via Santa we perceive a snake hewn in stone, and at the other corner a winged lion holding in its paw the snake's head. But at Venice we think far more of Shakespeare's immortal Shylock than of these historical personages who have long since lain mouldering in their graves. And when we cross the Rialto, we seek him everywhere and fancy that he must be standing behind some pillar clothed in his long Jewish gabardine, with a distrustful and calculating expression of countenance, and occasionally we imagine we hear him crying out in his husky voice, "three thousand ducats—well."

I at any rate, peripatetic dream-hunter as I am, looked about on the Rialto to see if I could spy out Shylock. 'I might have been the bearer of good news, such as that of my Parisian Lord Shylock becoming the mightiest peer in Christendom after being decorated by their Catholic Majesties with the order of Isabella, founded in memory of the Moors' and Jews' expulsion from Spain. But he was not to be found on the Rialto, and I settled to go in search of my old friend to the synagogue. Here the Jews were just celebrating the feast of Passover looking like a congregation of ghosts as they stood there in their white scarves, mysteriously bowing their heads. The poor Jews had stood there since the early morning fasting and praying, having taken nothing since the previous evening. Prior to this they had besought the pardon of their friends for any possible offence they might have given them throughout the year, in order that they in like measure might receive God's pardon for their sins ;—this is a beautiful custom and strangely enough we find it practised by those very people who have remained strangers to the gospel of Christ.

Unfortunately I cannot withhold a discovery which I made whilst in search of old Shylock among these pale-faced suffering Jews. I had that same day visited the lunatic asylum at San

Carlo, and now at the synagogue I perceived
in the Jews' faces that same strange, half-
staring, half-restless, half-sly, half-cunning, half-
timid expression, which shortly before I had
noticed in the lunatics at San Carlo. This
indescribably strange look did not so much
portend absence of mind as the supremacy of
a fixed idea. Is it possible that the belief in
that God of thunder preached by Moses has
become the fixed idea of an entire nation,
which refuses to swerve from its belief in spite
of the strait waistcoat and the shower bath
which have been administered to it for the
past two thousand years ;—much as that mad
lawyer whom I saw at San Carlo, and who
would not be persuaded that the sun was not a
cheese and that its beams were not maggots,
one of which was eating its way into his
brain !

I have no desire to question the value of
such a fixed idea. I only wish to say that its
exponents are too weak to retain the mastery
over their idea, and are weighed down by it
until they are past cure. What martyrdom
have they not already suffered for the sake of
this idea ! What greater martyrdom may there
not yet be in store for them ? I shudder at
the thought, and a great pity thrills through

my frame. During the whole of the middle ages down to the present day the dominant belief was not in direct opposition to the idea which Moses gave the Jews, by which he bound them in holy words and with which he circumcised them. They did not actually differ from Christians or Mahometans nor did they preach a different doctrine; they only interpreted it differently and gave it another name. But if ever Satan in the garb of that wicked pantheism, from which may all the saints of the Old and New Testament as well as the Koran defend us—if ever Satan gain the upper hand, then the poor Jews will have to suffer a persecution which will far outweigh any of their previous sufferings.

.   .   .   .   .   .

I could not see Shylock, though I looked about on every side in the synagogue at Venice. And yet I fancied he must be hiding under one of those white scarves, praying with more fervour than his fellow-believers, and sending up his prayers with wild passion— almost delirium—to the throne of Jehovah, the stern God! I did not see him. But towards evening, when, according to the belief of the Jews, the gates of heaven are closed and no prayer can gain admission, I heard a voice swimming in such tears as are never shed by mortals . . . it was a sobbing which might have moved a stone . . . they were groans such as could only be produced from a heart which had buried away in its depths the martyrdom suffered by an entire persecuted race for the length of eighteen hundred years . . . it was the death-throe of a soul sinking down in its prostration at heaven's gate . . . and this seemed to me a familiar voice, and I fancied I had heard it before calling out in its agony,

"Jessica ! my child !"

COMEDIES *

* See pp. 184–185 for Heine's explanation why he only quotes passages from Shakespeare's Comedies, without further elucidation of each play taken separately.

COMEDIES

MIRANDA.

(THE TEMPEST—*Act III., Scene I.*)

Ferdinand.

Wherefore weep you ?

Miranda.

At mine unworthiness that dare not offer
What I desire to give ; and much less take
What I shall die to want.   But this is trifling ;
And all the more it seeks to hide itself,
The bigger bulk it shows.   Hence, bashful cunning !
And prompt me, plain and holy innocence !
I am your wife if you will marry me ;
If not, I'll die your maid : to be your fellow
You may deny me ; but I'll be your servant,
Whether you will or no.

Ferdinand.

       My mistress dearest ;
And I thus humble ever.

Miranda.

          My husband then ?

Ferdinand.

Ay with a heart as willing
As bondage e'er of freedom : here's my hand.

TITANIA.

(MIDSUMMER NIGHT'S DREAM—*Act II., Scene III.*)
[*Enter Titania with her train.*

Titania.

Come now, a roundel and a fairy song;
Then for the third part of a minute hence;
Some to kill cankers in the musk-rose buds;
Some war with rere-mice for their leathern wings,
To make my small elves coats; and some keep back
The clamorous owl, that nightly hoots and wonders,
At our quaint spirits, sing we now asleep;
Then to your offices and let me rest.

PERDITA.

(THE WINTER'S TALE—*Act IV., Scene III.*)

Perdita.

Come, take your flowers:
Methinks I play as I have seen them do
In Whitsun pastorals; sure this robe of mine
Does change my disposition.

Florizel.

What you do
Still betters what is done. When you speak sweet
I'd have you do it ever; when you sing,
I'd have you buy and sell so; so give alms;
Pray so; and for the ordering your affairs
To sing them too; when you do dance I wish you,
A wave o' the sea, that you might ever do
Nothing but that; move still, still so,

And own no other function ; each your doing
So singular in each particular,
Crowns what you're doing in the present deeds,
That all your acts are queen's.

IMOGEN.

(CYMBELINE—*Act II., Scene II.*)

Imogen.

> Gods !
From fairies and the tempters of the night,
Guard me, beseech ye !

[*Sleeps. Jachimo comes from the trunk.*

Jachimo.

The crickets sing and man's o'erlaboured sense
Repairs itself by rest.   Our Tarquin thus
Did softly press the rushes, ere he wakened
The chastity he wounded.—Cytherea,
How bravely thou becom'st thy bed ! fresh lily !
And whiter than the sheets !   That I might touch !
But kiss ; one kiss !   Rubies unparagoned,
How dearly they do't !—'Tis her breathing that
Perfumes the chamber thus ; the flame o' the taper
Bows towards her ; and would underpeep her lids,
To see the enclosèd lights, now canopied
Under these windows, white and azure, laced
With blue of Heaven's own tinct.

JULIA.

(THE TWO GENTLEMEN OF VERONA—*Act IV., Scene II.*)

Julia.

How many women should do such a message ?
Alas, poor Proteus thou hast entertained

A fox to be the shepherd of thy lambs !—
Alas, poor fool ! why do I pity him,
That with his very heart despiseth me ?
Because he loves her he despiseth me ;
Because I love him, I must pity him.
This ring I gave him when he parted from me,
To bind him to remember my good-will :
And now am I—unhappy messenger—
To plead for that which I would not obtain ;
To carry that which I would have refused ;
To praise his faith which I would have dispraised.
I am my master's true-confirmèd love ;
But cannot be true servant to my master,
Unless I prove false traitor to myself.
Yet will I woo for him ; but yet so coldly,
As heaven it knows, I would not have him speed.

SILVIA.

(THE TWO GENTLEMEN OF VERONA—*Act IV., Scene IV.*)

Silvia.

Here, youth, there is my purse ; I give thee this
For thy sweet mistress' sake, because thou lov'st her,
Farewell.

Julia.

And she shall thank you for't if e'er you know her
　　　　　　　[*Exit Silvia with attendants.*
A virtuous gentlewoman, mild and beautiful,
I hope my master's suit will be but cold,
Since she respects my mistress' love so much.
Alas ! how love can trifle with itself !
Here is her picture ; let me see ; I think
If I had such a tire this face of mine
Were full as lovely as is this of hers ;

And yet the painter flattered her a little,
Unless I flatter with myself too much.
Her hair is auburn, mine is perfect yellow ;
If that be all the difference in his love,
I'll get me such a coloured periwig.
Her eyes are grey as glass ; and so are mine ;
Ay, but her forehead's low and mine's as high.
What should it be that he respects in her
But I can make respective in myself?

HERO.

(Much Ado about Nothing—*Act IV., Scene I.*)

Friar Francis.

Lady, what man is he you are accused of?

Hero.

They know that do accuse me ; I know none :
If I know more of any man alive
Than that which maiden modesty doth warrant,
Let all my sins lack mercy !—Oh, my father,
Prove you that any man with me conversed
At hours unmeet, or that I yesternight
Maintained the change of words with any creature,
Refuse me, hate me, torture me to death.

BEATRICE.

(Much Ado about Nothing—*Act III., Scene I.*)

Hero.

But nature never framed a woman's heart
Of prouder stuff than that of Beatrice ;
Disdain and scorn ride sparkling in her eyes,
Misprising what they look on ; and her wit

Values itself so highly, that to her
All matter else seems weak; she cannot love,
Nor take no shape nor project of affection,
She is so self-endeared.

. . . . .

Ursula.

Sure—sure such carping is not commendable.

Hero.

No, nor to be so odd, and from all fashions
As Beatrice is, cannot be commendable;
But who dare tell her so? If I should speak,
She'd mock me into air; oh, she would laugh me
Out of myself, press me to death with wit!
Therefore let Benedick, like covered fire,
Consume away in sighs, waste inwardly;
It were a better death than die with mocks,
Which is as bad as die with tickling.

HELENA.

(ALL'S WELL THAT ENDS WELL—*Act I., Scene III.*)

Helena.

Then, I confess,
Here on my knee, before high heaven and you,
That before you and next unto high heaven
I love your son :—
My friends were poor but honest; so's my love;
Be not offended; for it hurts not him,
That he is loved of me: I follow him not,
By any token of presumptuous suit,
Nor would I have him till I do deserve him :
Yet never know how that desert should be.
I know I love in vain, strive against hope;

Yet in this captious and intenible sieve,
I still pour in the waters of my love,
And lack not to lose still; thus Indian-like,
Religious in mine error, I adore
The sun that looks upon his worshipper,
But knows of him no more.   My dearest Madam,
Let not your hate encounter with my love,
For loving where you do.

CELIA.

(AS YOU LIKE IT—*Act I., Scene II.*)

Rosalind.

From henceforth I will coz and devise sports.   Let me see; what think you of falling in love?

Celia.

Marry.   I prithee do, to make sport withal; but love no man in good earnest; nor do further in sport neither than with safety of a pure blush thou may'st in honour come off again.

Rosalind.

What shall be our sport then?

Celia.

Let us sit and mock the good housewife Fortune from her wheel, that her gifts may henceforth be bestowed equally.

Rosalind.

I would we could do so; for her benefits are mightily misplaced; and the beautiful blind woman doth most mistake in her gifts to women.

Celia.

Tis true; for those that she makes fair she scarce makes honest; and those that she makes honest, she makes very ill-favoured.

ROSALIND.

(As You Like it—*Act III., Scene II.*)

Celia.

Didst thou hear these verses?

Rosalind.

Oh yes, I heard them all and more too; for some of them had in them more feet than the verses would bear.

Celia.

That's no matter; the feet might bear the verses.

Rosalind.

Ay, but the feet were lame, and could not bear themselves without the verse, and therefore stood lamely in the verse.

Celia.

But didst thou hear without wondering how thy name should be hanged and carved upon the trees?

Rosalind.

I was seven of the nine days out of the wonder before you came; for look here what I found on a palm-tree; I was never so be-rhymed since Pythagoras' time, that I was an Irish rat, which I can hardly remember.

OLIVIA.

(TWELFTH NIGHT—*Act I., Scene V.*)

Viola.

Good Madam, let me see your face.

Olivia (unveiling).

Have you any commission from your lord to negotiate with my face ? You are now out of your text ; but we will draw the curtain and show you the picture. Look you, Sir, such a one I was this present ; is't not well done ?

Viola.

Excellently done, if God did it all.

Olivia.

'Tis in grain, Sir, 'twill endure wind and weather.

Viola.

'Tis beauty truly blent, whose red and white
Nature's own sweet and cunning hand laid on.
Lady, you are the cruellest she alive,
If you will lead these graces to the grave
And leave the world no copy.

VIOLA.

(TWELFTH NIGHT—*Act II., Scene IV.*)

Viola.

My father had a daughter, loved a man,
As it might be perhaps, were I a woman,
I should your lordship.

Duke.

And what's her history ?

Viola.

A blank, my lord.   She never told her love,
But let concealment like a worm i' the bud
Feed on her damask cheek ; she pined in thought ;
And with a green and yellow melancholy,
She sat like Patience on a monument,
Smiling at grief.   Was not this love indeed ?
We men may say more, swear more ; but indeed
Our shows are more than will ; for still we prove
Much in our vows but little in our love.

Duke.

But died thy sister of her love, my boy ?

Viola.

I am all the daughters of my father's house,
And all the brothers too.   .   .   .

MARIA.

(TWELFTH NIGHT—*Act I., Scene III.*)

Sir Andrew.

Fair lady, do you think you have fools in hand ?

Maria.

Sir, I have not you by the hand.

Sir Andrew.

Marry, but you shall have, and here's my hand.

Maria.

Now, Sir, thought is free.   I pray you bring your hand
to the buttery bar, and let it drink.

Sir Andrew.

Wherefore, sweet-heart ?   What's your metaphor ?

Maria.

It's dry, Sir.

ISABELLA.

(MEASURE FOR MEASURE—*Act II., Scene IV.*)

Angelo.

Admit no other way to save his life, —
As I subscribe not that, nor any other,
But in the loss of question—that you, his sister,
Finding yourself desired of such a person,
Whose credit with the judge or own great place,
Could fetch your brother from the manacles
Of the all-binding law ; and that there were
No earthly mean to save him, but that either
You must lay down the treasures of your body
To this supposed, or else to let him suffer ;
What would you do ?

Isabella.

As much for my poor brother as myself ;
That is, were I under the terms of death,
Th' impression of keen whips I'd wear as rubies,
And strip myself to death as to a bed,
That long I have been sick for, ere I'd yield
My body up to shame.

PRINCESS OF FRANCE.

(Love's Labour's Lost—*Act IV., Scene I.*)

Costard.

God dig-you-den-all ! Pray you which is the head lady ?

Princess.

Thou shalt know her, fellow, by the rest that have no
heads.

Costard.

Which is the greatest lady, the highest ?

Princess.

The thickest and the tallest.

Costard.

The thickest and the tallest ! it is so ; truth is truth.
An your waist, mistress, were as slender as my wit,
One o' these maid's girdles for your waist should be fit.
Are not you the chief woman ? You are the thickest
here.

THE ABBESS.

(Comedy of Errors—*Act V., Scene I.*)

Abbess.

And thereof came it that thy man was mad.
The venom-clamours of a jealous woman
Poison more deadly than a mad-dog's tooth.
It seems his sleeps were hindered by thy railing ;
And therefore comes it that his head is light.
Thou say'st his meat was sauced by thy upbraidings ;
Unquiet meals make ill digestions ;
Thereof the raging fire of fever bred ;

And what's a fever but a fit of madness?
Thou say'st his sports were hindered by thy brawls:
Sweet recreation barred what doth ensue
But moody moping and dull melancholy,
Kinsman to grim and comfortless despair;
And at her heels a huge infectious troop
Of pale distemperatures and foes to life?
In food, in sport and life-preserving rest
To be disturbed would mad or man or beast;
The consequence is then thy jealous fits
Have scared thy husband from the use of wits."

MISTRESS PAGE.

(MERRY WIVES OF WINDSOR—*Act II., Scene II.*)

Mistress Quickly.

That were a jest indeed!—they have not so little grace
I hope!—that were a trick indeed! But Mistress Page
would desire you to send her your little page, of all loves.
Her husband has a marvellous infection to the little page;
and truly Master Page is an honest man. Never a wife in
Windsor leads a better life than she does; do what she
will, say what she will, take all, pay all, go to bed when she
list, rise when she list, all is as she will; and truly she
deserves it; for if there be a kind woman in Windsor, she
is one. You must send her your page; no remedy.

MISTRESS FORD.

(MERRY WIVES OF WINDSOR—*Act I., Scene III.*)

Falstaff.

No quipps now, Pistol.—Indeed I am in the waist two
yards about; but I am now about no waste; I am about
thrift. Briefly, I do mean to make love to Ford's wife. I

spy entertainment in her; she discourses, she carves, she gives the leer of invitation. I can construe the action of her familiar style; and the hardest voice of her behaviour to be Englished rightly is, "I am Sir John Falstaff's!"

ANNE PAGE.

(Merry Wives of Windsor—*Act I., Scene I.*)

Anne.

Will't please your worship to come in, Sir?

Slender.

No, I thank you forsooth heartily; I am very well.

Anne.

The dinner attends you, Sir.

Slender.

I am not a-hungry, I thank you forsooth. Go, Sirrah, for all you are my man, go wait upon my cousin Shallow. (*Exit Simple.*) A justice of peace sometime may be beholden to his friend for a man.—I keep but three men and a boy yet, till my mother be dead. But what though? yet I live like a poor gentleman born.

Anne.

I may not go in without your worship. They will not sit till you come.

KATHARINE.

(Taming of the Shrew—*Act II., Scene I.*)

Petruchio.

Say that she rail; why then I'll tell her plain,
She sings as sweetly as a nightingale.

Say that she frown ; I'll say she looks as clear
As morning roses newly washed with dew.
Say she be mute and will not speak a word ;
Then I'll commend her volubility,
And say she uttereth piercing eloquence.
If she do bid me pack, I'll give her thanks
As though she bid me stay by her a week.
If she deny to wed, I'll crave the day
When I shall ask the banns and when be married.
But here she comes ; and now, Petruchio, speak.
(Enter Katharine.)
Good morrow, Kate ; for that's your name, I hear.

Katharine.

Well have you heard, but something hard of hearing ;
They call me Katharine that do talk of me.

Petruchio.

You lie in faith ; for you are called plain Kate,
And bonny Kate, and sometimes Kate the cursed.

CONCLUSION

In the preface to this collection of pictures I mentioned how Shakespeare became popular in England and Germany, and how occasionally there arose some understanding of his works. Unfortunately I am unable to give as glowing a report of the romance countries; in Spain to this day the poet is unknown. Italy possibly remains in voluntary ignorance in order to ward off any transalpine rivalry from her great poets; and France, the home of acknowledged taste and elegant manners, long imagined that the great Englishman received sufficient honour at her hands when she called him a clever barbarian, trying to mock as little as possible at his coarseness. However the political revolution which this country experienced was followed by a literary revolution possibly surpassing the former in terrorism, and on this occasion Shakespeare was raised to the skies. Certainly the French in their literary as in their political revolutions are never quite honest; in the one as in the other they sing the praises of any hero not for his

real worth, but for the momentary advantage
which may accrue to their cause by means of
such laudations. This is why we find them
one day singing the praises of what another
day they find they must deprecate and *vice
versa.* For the past ten years that section of
society which has taken part in the literary
revolution entertains the blindest admiration
for the name of Shakespeare. But it remains
very questionable whether the movement has
called forth in these men any really con-
scientious appreciation or even proper understanding. The French have too strong a
family likeness with one another; they have
too completely drunk in the conventional lie
with their mother's milk, to feel any great
liking or sympathy for that poet who breathes
forth the truth of nature in every word.
French writers have certainly for some time
past earnestly and unintermittently striven
after such naturalness; in very despair they
strip off as it were their conventional habiliments, showing themselves in terrible naked-
ness. . . . But some fashionable rag,
which in spite of this has still clung to them,
gives sign of their inherited artificiality and
calls forth an ironic smile on the part of the
German beholder. These writers always bring

to my mind those illustrations accompanying certain novels in which the immoral love affairs of the eighteenth century are represented. Instead of the gentlemen's and ladies' paradisiacal habiliments made after nature's pattern, the former retain their pigtails and the latter their high *coiffures* and high-heeled shoes.

It was not owing to direct criticism that the French got a certain insight into the great poet's mind; they obtained this indirectly by means of dramatic works, more or less copied from Shakespeare;—in this, Victor Hugo is pre-eminent. I do not mean that he is, in the generally accepted sense, a copyist of the great Englishman. Victor Hugo's genius must be placed in the front rank and we must admire his capacity to soar and to create; he can give expression to his thought, he is the greatest French poet, but the noisy whirlpool of the present age fills his Pegasus with strange timidity, causing it to turn away from those waters in which it sees reflections of the light of day. . . . It rather seeks refreshment from those neglected springs situated among the ruins of the past where once upon a time Shakespeare's winged steed slaked its immortal thirst. I do not know whether any clear water is to be found in these old springs half empty

and turbid; but there is more of muddy slime
than of the life-giving properties of that ancient
English Hippocrene. His poems are wanting in bright clearness and healthy harmony
. . . and occasionally I confess I have a
terrible suspicion that this Victor Hugo is the
ghost of an English poet of Elizabeth's best
period, a dead poet risen from the grave with
a bad grace, in order to write a few posthu-
mous works in another country and another
period, so as to escape the rivalry of the great
Shakespeare. Victor Hugo indeed greatly
reminds me of men like Marlow, Decker,
Haywood and others who resembled their
great contemporary in language and style, but
who were unlike him in penetrative power and
love of the beautiful, in his terrible and his
smiling grace, in his revelation of nature . . .
and alas! added to Marlow's, Decker's, and
Haywood's shortcomings, we find in Victor
Hugo one of still greater magnitude; he is
wanting in life. The former suffered from
superabundant heat, the blood circulated wildly
in their veins, and their poetical works were
written emanations of their life's history, of
their joys and their sorrows. But Victor Hugo,
greatly as I admire him, has for me, I confess, something dead, gloomy, spectral, some-

thing of a risen Vampyre. . . . He does not awaken our enthusiasm, he completely exhausts it. . . . He does not cast a poetic halo over our tumultuous feelings; he terrifies them with some ghastly caricature . . . death and ugliness are his curse.

Some time ago a young lady whom I know well, expressed herself in a very significant manner concerning Hugo's mania for the hideous. She said: I am reminded in Victor Hugo's muse of that strange princess who wished to marry the ugliest man, and with this intention proclaimed throughout the country that on a certain day all the specially deformed bachelors were to assemble at her palace as suitors. . . . She did indeed procure for herself an assemblage of cripples and caricatures; it might have been a gathering of the characters mentioned by Hugo in one of his works . . . but Quasimodo won the bride.

After Victor Hugo I mention Alexander Dumas; he also assisted towards the better understanding of Shakespeare in France. If Hugo, by means of his extravagance in the domain of the hideous, accustomed the French to require in the drama something more than a fine draping of the passions, Dumas occasioned in his compatriots a great liking for the natural expression of their passions. But with him the passions are all in all, and they usurp the place of pure poetry in his poetical works. This certainly made his writing more effective for the stage. In the representation of the passions he accustomed the public to Shakespeare's boldest flights; and those who had once enjoyed *Henry III.* and *Richard Darlington* did not complain of want of taste in *Othello* and *Richard III.* The reproach of plagiarism attributed to him by some was as absurd as it was unjust. Certainly Dumas occasionally borrowed something from Shakespeare in his passionate scenes, but Schiller appropriated things quite as boldly without incurring blame. And even Shakespeare borrowed to a large extent from his predecessors. Even this poet had to face the assertion of some crabbed pamphleteer who maintained that his best plays were borrowed from previous authors. On this ridiculous occasion Shakespeare is called a raven, adorning himself with a peacock's plumage. The Swan of Avon held his peace, possibly thinking in his immortal soul: 'I am neither raven nor peacock,' as he rocked himself carelessly on the blue waves of poetry, smiling up at heaven's golden thoughts, the stars.

CONCLUSION

Count Alfred de Vigny has also to be named here. This author, having a good knowledge of English, studied Shakespeare's works more carefully than any other. He translated some of the plays very efficiently, and this study had a very good influence on his own writings. We may assume that the Count de Vigny, with the sensible and critical taste so essentially his, studied Shakespeare's genius more than most of his countrymen attempted to do. But the talents of this man as well as his thought and feeling are chiefly engaged in examining the microscopically small, and owing to their elaborate delicacy his works are peculiarly precious. Therefore I can well imagine that he must sometimes have been startled at the forms of superhuman beauty which Shakespeare as it were chipped off from the great granite blocks of poetry. . . . He must have regarded them in surprised admiration, like a jeweller gazing at the colossal gates of the Florence Baptistry. Though these were the result of a single casting, they nevertheless look delicate and lovely as though carved like the finest jewelry.

If the French find it sufficiently difficult to enter into Shakespeare's tragedies, his comedies almost entirely pass their comprehension. The

poetry of passion they can grasp, they can
even up to a certain point understand the
truth of character-painting, for their hearts
have learned to throb wildly, passion is their
speciality, and with their analytic understanding they can dissect a given character into its
finest parts, and can foresee the phases through
which such a one will pass should it come into
juxtaposition with certain realities of life.   But
all this experimental knowledge is of little use
to them in the magic garden of Shakespeare's
comedies.   They lose their wits at the very
gates, their hearts can lead them nowhither,
and they do not possess the mysterious wand
by the very touch of which the castle would
fly open.   They gaze in amazement through
the golden bars as they perceive knights and
ladies, shepherds and shepherdesses, fools and
wise men, wandering about among high trees ;
they see the lover and his beloved reposing in
the shade talking tenderly to one another, they
behold some mythical creature rushing past,
possibly a stag with silver antlers or a shy
squirrel jumping out of the foliage and hiding
its head in the beautiful maiden's lap . . .
and they see mermaids with green hair and
glistening veils plunge forth from the brooks,
and suddenly the moon appears . . . and

then they hear a nightingale sing . . . and they shake their wise little heads at all this incredibly stupid stuff! Ah, yes! the French may possibly have wit to understand the sun, but not the moon, and still less the happy sobbing and sad rapture of nightingales' voices.

Indeed neither their empirical acquaintance with human passions, nor their positive world-wisdom are of the least use to the French when they attempt to understand the appearances and voices which meet their eyes and ears in the magic garden of Shakespeare's comedies. . . . Sometimes they imagine they see a human face which turns into a landscape on their approach, what they had taken for eyebrows was a hazel-bush, the nose turned into a rock, and the mouth was a small streamlet similar to those well-known lantern slides which we sometimes meet with. . . . And *vice versa* that which the unfortunate French took for an extraordinarily-shaped tree or for a strange stone becomes on closer observation a real and hugely expressive human countenance. If they take the greatest trouble to overhear a lovers' dialogue in the shade of the trees, they are placed in a yet more awkward position, . . . they hear well-known words, but these words have another meaning, and then they declare that these people know nothing of warm love, of the great passion. These lovers were offering one another by way of refreshment cleverly manufactured ice, instead of the inspiring wine of love . . . and they did not perceive that they were birds in fancy dress, talking a peculiar language which can only be learned in dreams or in very early childhood. . . . But the worst that can befall the French waiting at the gates of Shakespeare's comedies, is— the moment when a sportive west wind blows across one of the flower beds of that magic garden, bearing on its wings a delicious scent. . . . "What can *that* be?"

I must in justice mention a French author who showed some cleverness in copying Shakespeare's comedies, and who exhibited rare susceptibility for true poetry by the choice of his models. This is Alfred de Musset. Five years ago he composed several small dramas which entirely resemble Shakespeare's comedies in construction and manner. With French ease he has appropriated to himself the fancifulness, —not the humour,—with which they abound. We find in these pretty trifles no absence of tolerably correct though very flimsy poetry. It was only a pity that this young author had read not only the French but Byron's version of Shakespeare. This led him to affect an appearance of satiety and spleen common to this nobleman, that being the fashion among the young Parisians of his day. The rosiest youths and healthiest greenhorns declared that they had lost all capacity for enjoyment, they pretended to a hoary freezing of the soul, and got themselves up in dishevelled and lazy fashion.

Certainly since then poor *Monsieur Musset* has retrieved his error and he is no longer *blasé* in his poems ; but alas ! instead of affected ruin his poems now contain the far sadder traces of a real decay of body and mind. . . . Ah me ! this writer reminds me of those artificial ruins which used to be built in eighteenth century palace gardens, those freaks of childish fancy which arouse our gentle pity when they ultimately fall into decay and crumble away into actual ruin.

The French, as I have noted, are not very capable of entering into the spirit of Shakespeare's comedies, and among their critics I have found only one who had the faintest conception of their latent and mysterious power. Who is this one exception ? Gutzkow signalises the elephant as the *doctrinaire* among animals. And such a wise and very clumsy elephant has best succeeded in penetrating the indwelling spirit of Shakespeare's comedies. Indeed it is difficult to believe that it is *Monsieur Musset* who has been the most successful in criticising these graceful and sportive visions of the modern muse. For the admiration and information of the reader I here translate a passage from a work published by Ladvocat of Paris in 1822, and which is entitled, *De Shakespeare et de la poésie dramatique par F. Guizot :*

"These comedies of Shakespeare resemble neither those of Molière, Aristophanes, nor those of the Romans. With the Greeks and later on with the French, comedy arose by means of an unhampered but also careful study of actual life, and it was the aim of comedy to represent this on the stage. In the early period of art, comedy was distinguished from tragedy, and the more art progressed the more marked was this distinction. The reason of this is self-evident. Man's destiny and nature, man's passions, employments, character and the incidents of his life, have in them both serious and humorous elements, and these can be observed and represented as well in the one way as in the other. This two-sidedness of man's nature and of the world has opened two separate paths for dramatic composition, but whilst choosing one or the other for its arena art has never turned away completely from the representation of reality. Aristophanes may scourge with boundless play of imagination the wickedness and foolishness of the Athenians, Molière may himself criticise the faults of credulity avarice jealousy, pedantry, family-pride, *parvenu* vanity and even of virtue itself. What matters it that both poets treat of entirely different subjects,—that the one has depicted on the stage the whole of life and an entire nation; the other, episodes of private life, family life and the absurdities of the individual;—this difference in the subject-matter of comedy is a consequence of the difference in time, place and civilisation. . . . But the plays of Aristophanes as of Molière are always based on reality and the actual world. The customs and beliefs of their century, the wickedness and foolishness of their fellow-citizens, in fact the . nature and life of man, is that which kindles and sustains their poetic fancy. Comedy is therefore a product of the world which surrounds the poet, and it approaches far more closely than tragedy the outward manifestations of reality. . . .

"Not so with Shakespeare. In his days in

England, nature and human destiny, the subject matter of dramatic art, had not yet received this distinction and classification at its hands. The poet, desiring to reproduce these on the stage, regarded them in their completeness with all their accompanying admixtures and contrasts; and public taste was not offended by such an action on his part. Comedy, this portion of human reality, might be made use of wherever truth demanded or suffered its presence, and it was quite homogeneous to English civilisation that tragedy, whilst appropriating something of comedy, did not thereby lose the dignity of truth. This being the condition of the stage and of public taste, how could actual comedy be represented? How could it take its place as a special form of composition and bear the distinguishing name of comedy? This was brought about by casting aside every fact in which the limits of that which is peculiar to comedy were neither observed nor acknowledged. This form of comedy did not restrict itself to the representation of certain manners and minutely described characters, nor did it seek to pourtray men in a ridiculous though true fashion. It became a phantastic and romantic work of imagination, a harbour for all those delightful impossibilities which a careless or fickle fancy weaves into a texture, in order to produce all manner of gay combinations which enliven and interest our imagination without exactly appealing to the verdict of common sense. Pleasing pictures, surprises, merry intrigues, amazed curiosity, disappointed hopes, misunderstandings and amusing actions which induce men to assume a disguise, formed the material of these harmless kaleidoscopic plays. The composition of the Spanish plays which were beginning to find favour in England made suitable settings and patterns for these plays, and could easily be adapted to those chronicles and romances, those French and Italian stories which, like the stories of chivalry, were much appreciated by the public. We can imagine that Shakespeare's attention was attracted at an early age by this rich mine of romance and ethereal kind of poetry. Nor does it surprise us that he, with his fresh and glowing imagination, loved to hover about those materials outside the domain of the strictest common-sense, from which he could produce every kind of serious and strong effect at the expense of probability. This poet, whose mind and whose fingers worked with equal ardour and whose manuscripts bore scarcely any traces of correction, must have found special pleasure in these kaleidoscopic plays, full of freedom and adventure, in which his manifold faculties could be manifested without exertion. He could pour all his experiences into his comedies, and indeed he did this without the addition of that logical combination which could never be adapted to a system such as his, in which every part of a composition is made subordinate to the whole and in which every particular manifests the depth, greatness and unity of the work. It would be difficult to find in Shakespeare's tragedies any conception, situation, act of passion, measure of guilt or of virtue, which might not in equal measure be found in his comedies. But what in his tragedies falls into abysmal depths, what proves terrible in its overwhelming consequences, what follows a strict rule of cause and effect, that in his comedies is scarcely dwelt on and only becomes apparent for a moment in order to bring about some passing effect and to turn as quickly into some new combination."

Verily this "elephant" is right. The spirit pervading Shakespeare's comedies may be likened to a gay butterfly flying from flower to flower and seldom touching the domain of reality. We can only express a decided opinion about Shakespeare's comedies in comparison

CONCLUSION

with those realistic forms of comedy natural to
the ancients and to the French.

I pondered long last night over the problem
whether it be possible to give any positive explanation of the spirit pervading Shakespeare's
comedies. I fell asleep after much ruminating,
and dreamed that I was sailing by starlight in
a tiny boat on a lake of great magnitude
where many barges, filled with masked people,
musicians and torches passed by, with sounds
and bright lights, now approaching now re-
ceding. I saw garbs of every period and
nation, Greek tunics of ancient times, knights'
cloaks of the middle ages, oriental turbans,
shepherd hats with flying streamers, weird
shapes of wild and of tame animals. . . .
Sometimes a well-known form greeted me
. . . sometimes beloved philosophers bowed
as they passed by . . . but all this speedily
vanished, and whenever I listened to a happy
song, issuing from one of the passing barges, it
was soon lost in silence, and instead of merry
fiddles I heard the melancholy bugles of
another barge. . . . Sometimes both of
these together were borne across to me on the
wings of the night wind, and then delicious
harmonies ensued from these mingled notes.
. . . The waters sounded pleasantly and

were tinged with magic reflections from the torches, and the bright pleasure boats with their strangely masked crew sailed on surrounded by light and music. . . . A lovely woman standing at the helm of one of the barges called out to me in sailing by : " well, friend, do you want to define the spirit pervading Shakespeare's comedies ? " I do not know whether I assented, but the beautiful woman immediately dipped her hand into the water, dashing some of the glittering spray on to my face so that I awakened to a peal of universal laughter.

Who was the lovely woman who made fun of me in my dreams ? She bore a gay cap and bells on her ideally beautiful head, a white satin dress with flying ribbons was draped around her slender form, and in her bosom she wore a blooming thistle. Perhaps she was the goddess of fancy, that strange muse, who was present with her kisses at the births of Rosalind, Beatrice, Titania, Viola and by what other names these lovely children of Shakepeare's comedies may be called. Possibly in kissing them she bestowed on these gay young heads all her moods, fancies, and whims, and *that* may have influenced their hearts. The women of Shakespeare's comedies resemble the men ;—their passions are free from that terrible earnestness, that fatalistic necessity which are manifested in his tragedies. Here also Cupid wears a bandage across his eyes and he bears in his hand a quiver with arrows. But in his comedies the arrows contain more feathers than poisoned darts, and the tiny god sometimes winks roguishly from beneath his bandage. Even the flames burn less than they glitter, yet they are flames, and love bears the character of truth in Shakespeare's comedies as in his tragedies. Yes, truth is always the characteristic mark of Shakespeare's love in whatsoever form it may appear, whether it be represented by Miranda, Juliet, or even Cleopatra.

In mentioning these names more casually than of set purpose I may remark that they typify the three most important forms of love. Miranda's love does not need historical influences in order to attain its highest ideal, it is the flower springing from virgin soil from a land where only spirits dwell. Ariel's songs have formed her heart, and sensuality has never appeared to her in any other form than in that of the detestably ugly Caliban. Therefore the love with which Ferdinand inspires her is not exactly an artless love, but one of

blissful simplicity of primitive almost awful
purity. Juliet's love as well as her surroundings and the period at which she lived, belong
rather to mediæval romance approaching the
renaissance period. It is bright as the court
of the Scaligers and strong as the noble families
of Lombardy who, with their infusion of German blood could love as strongly as they could
hate. Juliet represents the love of a youthful
somewhat turbulent, but sound and healthy
period. She is filled with the passionate
ardour and strong belief of such a time, and
even the cold decay of the tomb cannot van-
quish her confidence or extinguish her love.
But our Cleopatra represents the love of a
sickly civilisation, of a beautiful time whose
loveliness is fading away, and which adorns
itself with artificially curled and scented locks
containing many a grey hair ; of a time all the
more anxious to drink up the contents of a
cup the emptier that cup becomes. There is
neither faith nor fidelity in this love but it is
none the less warm and wild for that. The
impatient woman knowing in her anger that
this fire cannot be quenched pours oil on to
the flames, throwing herself upon them in
bacchanalian mood. She is a coward at heart
driven on by her love of destruction. Love is

always a kind of madness more or less beautiful, but in the case of this Egyptian queen it develops into the most terrific insanity . . . her love is a raging comet madly dashing around the firmament with its tail of fire, frightening if not wounding all the stars as it goes upon its course, and at the end exploding miserably like a rocket which bursts into a thousand sparks.

Yes, beautiful Cleopatra, we may liken thee to a terrific comet, and thou hast ruined thy contemporaries as well as thyself. . . . With Antony the old heroic Roman period comes to a miserable end.

But to what can I compare you, O Juliet and Miranda? Again I search the heavens for your prototype. Possibly it is hidden behind the stars too far off to reach my sight. Perhaps if the scorching sun possessed the moon's tenderness I might compare thee to the sun, O Juliet! Perhaps if the tender moon possessed the sun's heat I might compare thee to the moon, O Miranda!

Butler & Tanner, The Selwood Printing Works, Frome, and London.